Emily Harvale l
– although she
French Alps ... or   ...e that
has several mont   . Emily loves
snow almost as mu   ...s sne loves Christmas.

Having worked in the City (London) for several years, Emily returned to her home town of Hastings where she spends her days writing ... and wondering if it will ever snow.

You can contact her via her website, Facebook or Instagram.

There is also a Facebook group where fans can chat with Emily about her books, her writing day and life in general. Details can be found on Emily's website.

Author contacts:
www.emilyharvale.com
www.twitter.com/emilyharvale
www.facebook.com/emilyharvalewriter
www.instagram.com/emilyharvale

***

Scan the code above to see all Emily's books on Amazon

Also by this author

The Golf Widows' Club
Sailing Solo
Carole Singer's Christmas
Christmas Wishes
A Slippery Slope
The Perfect Christmas Plan
Be Mine
It Takes Two
Bells and Bows on Mistletoe Row

Lizzie Marshall series:
Highland Fling – book 1
Lizzie Marshall's Wedding – book 2

Goldebury Bay series:
Ninety Days of Summer – book 1
Ninety Steps to Summerhill – book 2
Ninety Days to Christmas – book 3

Hideaway Down series:
A Christmas Hideaway – book 1
Catch A Falling Star – book 2
Walking on Sunshine – book 3
Dancing in the Rain – book 4

Hall's Cross series
Deck the Halls – book 1
The Starlight Ball – book 2

Michaelmas Bay series
Christmas Secrets in Snowflake Cove – book 1
Blame it on the Moonlight – book 2

Lily Pond Lane series
The Cottage on Lily Pond Lane – four-part serial
Part One – New beginnings
Part Two – Summer secrets
Part Three – Autumn leaves

Part Four – Trick or treat
Christmas on Lily Pond Lane
Return to Lily Pond Lane
A Wedding on Lily Pond Lane
Secret Wishes and Summer Kisses on Lily Pond Lane

Wyntersleap series
Christmas at Wynter House – Book 1
New Beginnings at Wynter House – Book 2
A Wedding at Wynter House – Book 3
Love is in the Air – spin off

Merriment Bay series
Coming Home to Merriment Bay – Book 1
(four-part serial)
Part One – A Reunion
Part Two – Sparks Fly
Part Three – Christmas
Part Four – Starry Skies
Chasing Moonbeams in Merriment Bay – Book 2
Wedding Bells in Merriment Bay – Book 3

Seahorse Harbour series
Summer at my Sister's – book 1
Christmas at Aunt Elsie's – book 2
Just for Christmas – book 3
Tasty Treats at Seahorse Bites Café – book 4
Dreams and Schemes at The Seahorse Inn – book 5
Weddings and Reunions in Seahorse Harbour – book 6

Clementine Cove series
Christmas at Clementine Cove – book 1
Broken Hearts and Fresh Starts at Cove Café – book 2
Friendships Blossom in Clementine Cove – book 3

Norman Landing series
Saving Christmas – book 1
A not so secret Winter Wedding – book 2
Sunsets and surprises at Seascape Café-book 3
A Date at the end of The Pier – book 4

ISBN 978-1-909917-93-4

Published by Crescent Gate Publishing

Print edition published worldwide 2023
E-edition published worldwide 2023

Cover design by JR and Emily Harvale

Acknowledgements

My grateful thanks go to the following:

My webmaster, David Cleworth who does so much more than website stuff.
My cover design team, JR.
Luke Brabants. Luke is a talented artist and can be found at: www.lukebrabants.com
My wonderful friends for their friendship and love. You know I love you all.
All the fabulous members of my Readers' Club. You help and support me in so many ways and I am truly grateful for your ongoing friendship. I wouldn't be where I am today without you.
My Twitter and Facebook friends, and fans of my Facebook author page. It's great to chat with you. You help to keep me (relatively) sane!

To all the wonderful members of my Facebook group. Thank you for your continued support and friendship.

Emily Harvale

That Mistletoe Moment

CRESCENT GATE PUBLISHING

MAP KEY – BETANCOURT BAY

1) **Lookout Point** – At **310 feet**, this is the highest point on the white cliffs around Betancourt Bay. You can see Locke Isle from here while seated on the bench, and on a very clear day, even the coast of France. **Lookout Steps** lead down to the sandy beach – but there are **300 steps**, so most people access the beach farther along, where the cliff paths aren't so steep and there are fewer steps.

2) **Sunnycliff Cottage** - **James and Margaret Hart** live here. They have two daughters, **Fiona** and **Naomi**. Fiona lives in Folkestone with her boyfriend. Naomi is single and lives in Lewisham (London) where she rents a flat with two friends.

3) **Willow Cottage** – Home to **Malorie Blackwell**, a reflexologist.

4) **Seaview Cottage** – **Laurence Lake** lives here. He's a successful author of several cosy crime books.

5) **Rosehip Cottage** – **Jean and**

Victor Mills live here. Their four children, **Tom, Rob, Zoe and Tara** have all moved away but they come home for high days and holidays.

6) **Betancourt** – Ancestral home to the Betancourt family which currently consists of **Archie Betancourt**, his second wife, **Bianca** (his first wife **Francesca**, died) and his two sons, **Grifforde (known as Griff)** and **Russell.**

7) **Mr and Mrs Bernard and Barbra Brimble's B & B** – **Barbra** describes herself as 'a people person'; people describe her as 'a nosy gossip' – but not to her face. She loves to sing, and often does, whether others want her to or not.

8) **Clifftop Farm** – Once part of the Betancourt's estate, but now a small holding owned by **Sandy and Sonia Grey**, most of the farmland having been sold-off by various Betancourts over the years. Sandy and Sonia are known for taking in all sorts of waifs and strays, both human and animal.

9) **The Royal Oak** pub – Although highly unlikely, legend has it that King Richard (The Lionheart) once sat beneath the ancient oak tree opposite the pub, on his way to join the Crusades. Owned and run by **Freddie Tollard** and his daughter, **Charlotte (Charlie)**

10) **The White House** – Home to **Simon and Patience (Pat) Eversley** and daughters **Grace** and **Hope** along with their dog, **Lady Elizabeth, known as Lady E**. The Eversleys run an Events company, **Eversley Events** from here.

11) The Rectory – **The Reverend Brian Copeland** and his wife **Daisy** live here.

12) **St Gabriel's Church** – with a bijou village hall attached. The church was built in 1086, the hall in 1946.

13) **Catkin Cottage** – Home to **Hanna Shaw**, an artist.

14) **Acorn Cottage** – Elderly sisters, **Rita and Vera Boot** have lived here all their lives.

15) **Bluebell Cottage** – **Greg Bishop** lives here. He owns a bookshop in Folkestone.

16) **Oak View Cottage** – **Molly Law** has recently inherited this cottage from her grandmother, **Millicent**. Molly lives in Folkestone with her parents, **Owen and Nikki**.

17) **Betancourt Bay Café** – Owned by **Derek Dunpole** and his (miserable) wife, **Doris**, who had much grander plans than running a café in a small village, as she constantly reminds her long-suffering husband.

18) **West Wood** – owned by the Betancourts but they allow the villagers to use it.

19) **East Wood** – also owned by the Betancourts, who allow the villagers access.

Wish you were here?

This new series is set in Betancourt Bay, a fictional, clifftop village a mile from Folkestone. I've, sort of, 'demolished' everything that currently occupies this space in real life, and 'built' Betancourt Bay there instead. Apologies for that, but it was a necessary evil in order for me to tell these stories.

In addition to this, I have added a few fictional things/places/businesses in Folkestone – like the slipway where the Locke Isle Ferry docks, among others, so please forgive me for that!

This series also links to my other new series, Locke Isle, which is set on the fictional island of Locke Isle, two miles off the Kent coast, and also partly in the real town of Folkestone.

So if you know Folkestone and the surrounding area, you may not entirely recognise it when you read these books...

With love,
Emily xx

One

Something had happened. Something monumental judging by the scene that met Grace Eversley and Lady Elizabeth, the family dog, when they returned from their early morning walk that bitterly cold December morning.

Lady E, a French Bulldog, sensed it before Grace and stuck her stubby nose in the air the moment Grace opened the pink front door of The White House, the spacious cottage Simon Eversley and his wife, Patience, known as Pat to all their friends, had called home since before Grace was born.

Pat and Simon had purchased the cottage in the tiny, clifftop village of Betancourt Bay shortly after their marriage thirty-seven years ago, and had retained its name, which it derived from its bright white façade. Pat had fallen in love with the cottage the moment she saw its leaded-light windows, but it was the window seats, ancient oak ceiling beams and the inglenook fireplaces in the kitchen, sitting room and dining room that stole her heart completely. Simon had fallen in love with it because Pat had, and both had intuitively known that this would be their forever-home. It was close to Pat's widowed mum, Joy Button, who lived in Folkestone less than a five-minute drive from the cottage, and far enough away from Simon's parents, who lived in Essex, and had never felt Pat was quite good enough for their only son, and were certain the marriage wouldn't last. They went to great pains to let that be known whenever possible, even after thirty-seven years.

Pat and Simon's daughters, Grace and her younger sister, Hope, had called their cosy home Candy Floss Cottage when they were children due to its pink front door, pink window frames and its chestnut-brown thatched roof. The Eversleys had discussed painting the door and windows a different colour over the years, but somehow it hadn't seemed right, and so The White House looked exactly the same now as it had decades before, from the outside at least. The inside had seen many changes since Pat and Simon first moved in.

The cottage was situated between The Royal Oak pub and The Rectory, the other side of which was St Gabriel's Church. Grace's maternal grandmother, Granny Joy, often joked that the family sat between saints and sinners, and it was sometimes difficult to tell which was which. A sentiment with which Freddie Tollard, the pub owner, wholeheartedly agreed; The Reverend Brian Copeland, not so much.

Grace shook off the worst of the rain that had settled on her coat and hair, before stepping into the hall. She hadn't taken an umbrella with her on the walk because the forecast hadn't mentioned rain but the heavens had opened as she and Lady E turned onto Folkestone Road. Luckily it was only a few steps from the corner of the road to The White House but her long, walnut-brown hair, tied into a French plait, was dripping wet beneath the lime green and red knitted bobble hat she wore. That, and her berry-red wool scarf had been Christmas stocking gifts from Granny Joy last year, along with matching gloves, but Grace preferred to wear the black leather gloves she had bought as a gift to herself.

Once inside, she placed her gloves on the hall table to dry beside the large, black, ceramic top hat where all the gloves were kept, and after removing her keys from the lock, she tossed those into the white, ceramic bowl shaped like a bow tie. She then removed

3

Lady E's lead and hung it on the hook near the front door before peeling off her sodden hat and shrugging off her lime green, winter coat, along with her scarf. She gave them all another shake prior to hanging them on the coat rack, leaving space between her wet garments and all the others hanging there. Grace was nothing if not considerate.

'What is it, Lady E?' Grace asked, kicking off her mud-splattered, black leather ankle boots, surprised to see that, instead of the dog's claws skittering down the hall and across the tiled floor of the kitchen as she dashed for her water bowl within seconds of her lead being removed, as was the custom after a walk, Lady E had stopped halfway along the wooden floor of the hall and was glancing back at Grace.

In response to Grace's question, Lady E gave a quick 'gruff', which Grace knew from experience was the dog's way of saying, 'Something's up. You go first and find out what. I'll follow when it's safe.'

Lady E wasn't the bravest of dogs, but then again, she was rather tiny so who could blame her? Grace's dad, Simon had always said it was because Lady E was a French Bulldog, and therefore expected to be pampered and protected, with which Grace's sister, Hope agreed. Hope also said it was because Lady E believed she was dog-aristocracy, or at the very least, a pedigree, and the entire Eversley family were merely there to serve her and keep her away from any unpleasantness. Sadly, although Lady E's mother was a French Bulldog, her father was of an indeterminate breed, and probably a mix of several judging by the look of him when the Eversleys had selected Lady E from a brood of puppies several Christmases ago. Grace and Pat had always believed that the reason Lady E 'hung back' if she sensed something unexpected or unusual was afoot, was simply because the dog was smart. Well, most of the time.

Now, Lady E's big 'bat ears' stood erect and her dark eyes shot a look along the hall to the kitchen and then back at Grace, and she angled her paws and her body slightly as if preparing to run.

Grace wasn't overly concerned. This was Betancourt Bay after all. Nothing really bad ever happened here, but after a second or two, it dawned on Grace that Lady E was right. Something was definitely up.

Other than Wizzard booming out *I Wish it Could be Christmas Every Day*, via Heart Xmas radio and the Google Nest Hub, silence emanated from the kitchen. And silence in the Eversley household, especially at this time of year, was unheard of ... so to speak, so Grace hurried along the hall to the kitchen, anxious to find out what had occurred during the forty-five minutes she and Lady E had been gone.

Grace could see that the myriad fairy lights decorating every available inch of the blackened oak beams, the kitchen shelves, and all the cupboards, twinkled as brightly as they had when she had left, so it wasn't a power cut. The aroma of coffee filled the air as it always did between the hours of seven a.m. and noon in the Eversley household, so it wasn't a caffeine shortage. It was far too early for Bert, their postman, as it was only fifteen minutes past nine and he never appeared until at least eleven a.m. and so no terrifyingly extortionate red bills had arrived, unless they'd been sent via email.

Grace couldn't think of anything that could justify the scene before her when she reached the kitchen doorway. Pat, Simon, and Hope all looked as if they were under a black magic spell as they sat motionless around the large, circular, pine kitchen table, each of them hugging a mug of still steaming coffee, as if their very lives depended on it.

Grace was about to speak but Hope beat her to it. Hope had her back to the doorway so Grace couldn't see her face but her solemn tone was far removed from her usual cheery one.

'The woman did say, "Money is no

object", so at least we'd make a killing.'

Pat shook her head and sighed. 'It's a massive undertaking, Hope, and we're already so busy.'

'I know. But looking on the bright side,' Hope said dryly, 'Grace will be over the moon.'

'That's true.' Pat gave a quick nod, followed by another lengthy sigh which was matched by Simon.

Grace spotted a furrow the size of the Suez Canal between her dad's dark brows. Okay, that might have been a slight exaggeration. Grace had been known to stretch the truth from time to time, even to herself. In fact, especially to herself. But her dad definitely did not look happy and neither did her mum.

'But it's the Betancourts,' Simon said, in a tone that sounded as if he were afraid of summoning up the devil at the mere mention of that name.

It had the opposite effect on Grace.

'The Betancourts!' she shrieked, racing into the kitchen and making her family jump. 'What about them? What's happened? Why do you all look as if Father Christmas has just died?'

'Grace!' Pat exclaimed, her right hand shooting to her chest. 'You almost gave me a heart attack. I didn't hear you come in.'

'Where's Lady E?' Simon questioned, glancing at the undisturbed water bowl, just as a skitter of claws announced the dog's arrival, followed by loud lapping and grunting as Lady E, now seemingly convinced she was safe, enjoyed her drink.

'How long have you been lurking there?' Hope asked, frowning almost as deeply as Simon had been.

'About five seconds,' Grace said. 'And I wasn't lurking.' Her gaze darted from one member of her family to another as she pulled out a kitchen chair and plonked herself down. 'Well? Is anyone going to fill me in? Why are you discussing the Betancourts?' She sucked in a sharp breath. 'Nothing bad's happened to Russell, has it? Or to any of them,' she hastily added.

'That depends on your definition of bad,' Hope sneered. 'As far as we know, Russell is fine and so are the rest of them, other than Bianca who believes the world as she knows it has come to an end.'

A small sigh of relief escaped Grace once she knew Russell and his dad, Archie, were okay. His elder brother, Griff, she couldn't care less about, nor his step mum, Bianca – although she wouldn't wish harm on either of them, of course.

She poured herself coffee from the pot sitting on the kitchen table into the

Christmas-themed mug that had been waiting there for her return, and adding milk from the equally Christmassy jug, asked, 'Oh? Why's that?'

Anything about the Betancourts intrigued her. Mainly because she had been in love with Russell Betancourt for as long as she could remember.

Her parents had hoped she would out-grow her infatuation and over the years they had frequently told her that it wasn't wise to believe one's self in love with someone since the age of eight. Grace believed it was Destiny. Hope told her it was plain stupidity. Granny Joy told her it would lead to trouble and probably end in tears. But Grace was undeterred.

And still in love with Russell Betancourt, at the age of thirty-four.

She had dated other men, just as Russell had dated other women, but no man could match up to Russell in Grace's eyes, and thankfully, he had remained unmarried. So far.

Hope grinned. 'That posh events company from London that Bianca has used to organise the Mistletoe Dance for the last god-knows-how-many-years has done the unthinkable and made the biggest blunder in the history of blunders by failing to book this year's event into its planning schedule. They were meant to arrive yesterday to get things started but they didn't turn up. When Bianca called to find out where they were, they told her they had no record of her booking, and used the 'new staff' excuse, apparently. She gave them a right earful, obviously, and reminded them they've organised the event for years, in response to which they told her, "not this year", and then hung up.'

'They hung up on Bianca Betancourt!' Grace couldn't believe her ears. 'Who told you all that?'

Hope laughed, Simon scowled, and Pat rolled her eyes.

'Bianca,' Pat said, followed by yet another sigh.

'Bianca *told* you that?' Grace cast a glance around the table, unable to take this news in.

'Yep,' Hope said. 'We had literally just got off the phone with her a few seconds before you returned. She was outraged, as you can imagine. I suggested Mum should do the same, but obviously our darling mother is far too kind-hearted to hang up on someone. Even Bianca Betancourt.'

'It would have been rude,' Pat said, looking as though she were wishing she had done precisely that.

'Bianca phoned here?' That was a first. 'So ... so what does that mean? Is she calling everyone to cancel?' Grace squeaked, like a mouse discovering the world had run out of cheese. 'Are you saying there's not going to be a Mistletoe Dance?'

The Mistletoe Dance was the annual event of the year on the Betancourt Bay calendar and everyone was invited. Everyone who lived in the clifftop village of Betancourt Bay, that is. It was one of those age-old traditions that had been passed down from generation to generation and none of the Betancourts had either wanted, or dared, to be the one to put a stop to it. One did try once apparently, and almost had a revolution on his hands when the entire population of the village turned up at the ornate iron gates of Betancourt with pitchforks and torches, or so the story went.

'And I don't mean the type of torches you find on your mobile phone,' Granny Joy had said when she regaled Grace and Hope with the story. 'I mean the burning kind, with oil and flames.'

Grace wasn't entirely sure she believed her grandmother, but as the population of the village only consisted of around forty people, give or take a few, and was probably even fewer in those days, the mob was hardly likely to have been terrifying.

It wasn't only the village residents who attended the event, of course. Invitations

11

went out months in advance to several prominent people from the surrounding towns and villages, together with all of the Betancourts' friends.

People said that recipients of the much-coveted invitation often placed the stylish, gold edged and gold embossed, white and green card on their mantlepieces, office desks, or somewhere equally visible, in the knowledge that others would be envious.

The Betancourts might not be as powerful as they once were, nor as wealthy as their ancestors had been, and they were no longer aristocracy thanks to the last Baron Betancourt having picked the wrong side, centuries earlier, and been fortunate that it was only his title and most of his land that had been taken and not his ancestral home, nor his head, but everyone in Kent and far beyond, wanted to attend at least one of their events. Preferably, the one on Christmas Eve.

The suggestion of there not being a Mistletoe Dance was unthinkable.

Hope grinned at Grace. 'Not unless Bianca can find another events company to step in at the last minute.'

'At this time of year and with only a little over two weeks until Christmas! She'll need a small miracle to do ... wait a minute!' Grace's eyes lit up as brightly as the myriad rows of fairy lights around the kitchen when the penny finally dropped. 'Did Bianca call and ask *us* to step in?' Grace could hardly contain her surprise. Or her excitement.

Eversley Events had existed for the last fifteen years, but not once had the Betancourts asked the Eversleys to as much as quote for an event they were holding at Betancourt, let alone for the Mistletoe Dance. Neither Hope nor Grace knew why the Betancourts ignored Eversley Events when it came to business, but they always had, and Pat and Simon had told their daughters years ago that the Eversleys would never work for the Betancourts even if that family ever did want to employ them.

'Let's just say ... we had a difference of opinion a long time ago,' Simon once told Grace and Hope, 'and leave it at that. They will never ask, so we'll never have to say no.'

Grace hadn't really understood, because although Bianca Betancourt looked down her nose at them, the woman did that to everyone, so Grace knew that her family wasn't singled out for Bianca's distain. But the Betancourts did hire other local businesses in and around Betancourt Bay to do various jobs for them – yet never Eversley Events, despite holding several grand parties at Betancourt throughout the year, not just the Mistletoe Dance.

In a way, that only added to the crush

Grace had on Russell Betancourt. She fancied the pair of them as a sort of Romeo and Juliet who were always destined to fall in love despite their families feuding.

Not that the Eversleys and the Betancourts had ever feuded, to her knowledge. In fact, when the first Mrs Betancourt was alive, long before Pat and Simon set up their own events business, both families got on fairly well.

Grace and Hope, together with the other children in the village, had often spent time with the Betancourt brothers, Griff and Russell in those days. They all swam in the sea during the long, hot, summers, or played cricket on the common near Lookout Point, or croquet on the manicured lawn at Betancourt during the annual Summer Fayre.

Grace had fallen in love with Russell the moment she believed she was old enough to know what romantic love was, which for her, was around the age of eight. Coincidently, that was also when Granny Joy had told her the tales of Camelot: of King Arthur, Guinevere, and Sir Lancelot, and of Ivanhoe, Rebecca and Rowena, and of Robin Hood and Maid Marian, which may have had something to do with Grace's sudden interest in heroic men – and love.

Russell was a year older than Grace, and

was the perfect hero with the same golden blond hair and deep blue eyes as his dad, Archie. Griff was two years older and the ideal villain with thick and unruly ebony hair, like his mum, Francesca's, and her equally dark and intense eyes. Both boys were tall, agile, strong for their years, and handsome even then. And both, like fine wine, had improved with age.

Grace had often daydreamed of Griff kidnapping her and of Russell riding to rescue her from Griff's evil intentions, and yet at night, when she slept, especially when she reached her teens, her dreams frequently reversed the roles, making Griff the rescuer. Those were more like nightmares.

More than once, Grace had caught Griff watching her and Hope attentively back then, as if there was something about the two sisters that he didn't entirely trust. Perhaps he thought they were after the family silver, and being the eldest son and therefore the one who would inherit Betancourt and all the family's possessions, he wanted to keep an eye on the village kids, and in particular, the Eversley sisters, for some reason.

Generally speaking though, Griff and Russell were friends with Grace and Hope. Griff did infuriate Grace sometimes because he liked to play practical jokes and often picked on her, whereas Russell was always the perfect gentleman, especially when they were all in their early teens.

Yet over the years, Grace had noticed that whenever her parents came face to face with Francesca and Archie Betancourt there was a slight tension in the air, as though the adults were all treading on eggshells. At first she thought it was simply because the Betancourts were, well, Betancourts, and her family were simply ordinary village folk. Pat was a stay-at-home mum, and Simon was a manager of a building society branch office in Folkestone. The Betancourts owned a stately home and a thriving auction house in London. But Pat Eversley had no truck with class or any of that nonsense, as she called it, so it clearly wasn't because she felt intimidated.

'We're all made of skin and bone,' Pat always maintained, 'and we're all born and we all die. No one should be considered 'better' simply because they have more money, or a seemingly important job. We're all equals.'

Grace had asked whether something had happened in the past to cause any friction between the families but Pat, Simon, and also Granny Joy had said that the past should be left where it was and would say no more than that.

Grace asked Russell if he knew, but all he

had done was shrugged and told her she was imagining it. When she eventually asked Griff, he gave her one of his intense looks and told her not to ask questions to which she might not like the answer. Naturally, she had pressed him on the matter, but he had told her it wasn't his place to say, and he refused to discuss it further.

And then everything had changed when Francesca Betancourt was diagnosed with pancreatic cancer a few days after Christmas the year that Russell had turned fifteen and Griff was just sixteen. She was gone within five weeks.

The entire village attended the funeral and Grace's heart broke for Russell and his family. He was devasted, as were Griff and Archie, and the three of them retreated behind the walls of Betancourt for several weeks.

Russell had always kept his feelings close to his chest and in many ways, he was a shy boy prior to his mum's death, but afterwards, he became even more tight-lipped and reticent.

Many people had said they expected Francesca's passing to hit Griff the hardest because he was extremely close to his mum and there was always that intensity about him and anything he did. He had certainly looked shell-shocked at the funeral and hadn't said a word to anyone.

Grace still remembered the first time she saw Griff a few weeks later. She was fourteen at the time, two years younger than Griff, and in place of the fun-loving, friendly, albeit slightly intense and extremely mischievous boy, was a sarcastic teenager who made it clear that no one mattered to him, apart from his brother and his dad.

Grace had heard via her parents, who had heard via the village grapevine, that both Griff and Russell would be going away to boarding school, and Archie would be spending more time away from home. It seemed none of them could bear to be at Betancourt without Francesca. It was the day before Griff was leaving, and even now, Grace could still see in her mind's eye, the look he gave her that day.

She had bumped into him on her way home from school – the school in Folkestone that both Griff and Russell had formerly attended. She attempted to offer some words of comfort, just as she had tried to do at the funeral, but Griff's response had shocked her.

On seeing Griff, she hadn't been sure what to say and had clearly made a mess of it, because he glared at her as she told him once again how sorry she was about Francesca and that he and Russell would be missed in the village once they left for boarding school.

He looked her up and down and his gaze seared her skin with its intensity, and then he smiled sardonically and said, 'As if you care, Grace. I think we'll both be glad to see the back of one another.' And with that, he had walked away.

Grace couldn't believe what had happened. It was true that she didn't like Griff as much as she did Russell, and she would be the first to admit that she had sometimes missed things Griff said to her in the past because her attention was focussed on Russell and not on Griff, but she had never actively disliked Griff, or shown him any animosity – until that day.

After that, Grace rarely saw either Russell or Griff but they, along with their dad, came home for the Mistletoe Dance. Most of the villagers assumed it would be cancelled that first year, but it was Francesca's dying wish that the dance would still be held. Christmas had always been her favourite time, and she had adored the Mistletoe Dance. Although it clearly broke the hearts of those she had left behind, they had honoured her wish. Relatives and friends had organised the event that year, and Archie, Griff and Russell had attended, albeit for only a matter of an hour or so. And in Griff's case, about fifteen minutes. All of them had left again on Christmas Day, and had gone to stay with relatives.

The following year, they stayed at Betancourt for longer, and the year after that, they stayed for one week, but Grace still only saw Russell and Griff at the Mistletoe Dance each time, and only briefly.

Russell was always polite and asked how she was; Griff merely scowled at her and nodded in a sort of greeting. But there was now a distance between the Betancourts and the rest of the villagers, and that distance wasn't helped by the arrival of Bianca.

Archie met Bianca, three and a half years after Francesca's death, and married her within a matter of weeks. That Christmas, it was Bianca who had organised the annual, Mistletoe Dance, or at least, had employed an events company in London to do so. And she had been doing that ever since, and the distance between the Betancourts and the residents of Betancourt Bay, had become greater.

In fact, Bianca appeared to actively encourage it, and Archie, Griff and Russell didn't seem to care. Griff and Russell had new friends. Friends who had more in common with them, according to Bianca. Friends from boarding school. Then friends from university. Then friends connected with work.

Both Griff and Russell lived and worked in London after university, and travelled all over the world for the family's auction house business, yet each year, they both came back to Betancourt for the Mistletoe Dance, no matter what, in honour of their mum.

Grace had always worried that one year, Russell would announce he was engaged, especially as he had sometimes brought the same woman home for more than two years running, but thankfully, he had remained single.

Griff never brought the same woman home twice, and he'd made it clear that marriage wasn't on his agenda.

Russell came home more frequently as the years passed, but Griff kept his visits to once a year – for the Mistletoe Dance, and he always left before New Year, whereas Russell extended his visits each time.

Whenever Grace and Russell met, he seemed pleased to see her and each time they spoke for longer than they had on the previous occasion.

Whenever Grace saw Griff, he scowled at her, and she soon grew into the habit of scowling back.

But in recent years, even if Russell brought a date with him to the Mistletoe Dance and home for the Christmas holidays, he seemed to make a beeline for Grace and her family. He always enquired how they all were and was keen to ask questions about Grace and her sister.

Griff's scowl had turned into a sardonic smile, like the one he had given Grace all those years before, but other than that, he paid her no attention, although he did always make an effort to talk to her parents, and also to Hope, which Grace found slightly irritating.

But other than checking out the latest beauty Griff had brought with him for the dance and the holidays – a different one each Christmas – Grace paid no attention to him. She was always far too busy talking, watching, admiring, and swooning over Russell to concern herself with Griff.

Although, she did always wish she could wipe that damn smile from Griff's handsome face. It seemed to grow wider and more sardonic every Christmas. The smile that is, not Griff's face, which, annoyingly had only grown more handsome over the years.

'That man gets better looking every time I see him,' Hope had pointed out last Christmas. 'Even you must agree he's hot.'

Grace had to reluctantly admit that Griff was rather sexy, in an arrogant and overbearing way.

But Griff still wasn't as handsome as

Russell, in Grace's eyes, and she was more than happy to let the other women in the village, including her own sister, swoon over Grifforde Betancourt.

This past year, Russell had been coming home to Betancourt more frequently and was, as always, polite and friendly when he and Grace met. Grace tried to make sure they met as often as possible and asked her parents and her sister, and even a few of the villagers, to ping her a text if they saw him. She pretended she needed to have a word with him about something or other. Luckily, no one ever asked what, or why she couldn't simply text him herself.

'You do realise,' Hope said, 'that some people might equate your behaviour to stalking, don't you?'

Grace tutted dismissively in response. 'I'm merely being friendly ... and attentive.'

Hope told her she was mad.

Pat and Simon continued to encourage her to date other men, which she still did from time to time, but none of them compared to Russell.

Granny Joy maintained that the infatuation would end in tears.

'It's not infatuation, Granny,' Grace rebuked her. 'I've been in love with Russell all my life!'

'Stuff and nonsense,' Granny Joy

replied. She had grown a little grumpy with age, and less inclined to join in with Grace's fantasies as she had once been. 'You only think you're in love with him. Your problem is you see the man as some sort of romantic hero instead of the real person he is, and you always have. You need to open your eyes, my darling, and look around. You might see someone far better suited to you than Russell Betancourt will ever be.'

But Grace took no notice.

Every year, she had been secretly wishing that Russell would ask her to be his date for the Mistletoe Dance. She knew that he wouldn't be home until the week before the dance, as usual, but this year, unlike all the previous years, Russell wasn't bringing a date with him. He had told her so the last time they had met, which was at a Bonfire Party at Lookout Point in November. Griff hadn't come home for that.

So, unless Russell had started dating someone since November, this year might be the year that Grace's Christmas wish would come true.

The fact that the Mistletoe Dance might not go ahead was definitely unthinkable.

But now, after all these years, Bianca Betancourt had asked the Eversleys to organise the Mistletoe Dance. Grace was determined her family would not say no.

Finally, she would get the opportunity to spend more time with Russell. And frankly, she couldn't wait.

Grace was so excited she would have been willing to organise the event for free. Her parents, and Hope made it clear that wasn't going to happen.

'I think we should charge them double,' Hope said, after Grace had begged and pleaded with them all to say yes, and vowed that she would do most of the work even if it meant being at Betancourt for twenty-four hours a day every day until Christmas Eve, the night of the Mistletoe Dance.

'We can't do that,' Simon said, never one to rip off a client. 'But as it is short notice, we can charge a little more than usual.'

'And Bianca will still be getting a bargain,' Pat said, somewhat grudgingly.

'If Grace gets her Christmas wish,' said Hope, as if she had been reading Grace's mind, 'the one she makes every year, then this will be the year Russell finally asks her to be his date for the dance. I wonder what Bianca will have to say about that. Her step son dating the help.'

'We're not 'help', Pat snapped, surprising both her daughters. 'We're just as good as the Betancourts and don't ever let anyone say otherwise.'

Hope pulled a face and grinned. 'Okay,

Mum. Calm down. All I'm saying is that Bianca might get more than she bargained for.'

'Amen to that!' Grace said, laughing joyfully, and then she let out a loud, swoony sigh. 'I'm going to make sure there's plenty of mistletoe because, even if Russell doesn't ask me to be his date, I'm going to get a kiss from him this Christmas if it's the last thing I do. And I don't care what Granny says.'

'What has Granny said?' Hope asked.

Grace cleared her throat. 'Nothing important.' She tossed her French plait over her left shoulder and stuck out her chin. 'Now will you please phone Bianca, Mum, and tell her the good news! Eversley Events will be delighted to organise this year's Mistletoe Dance. And it will be the best one the Betancourts and their guests have ever seen.'

Two

'You'll do it?' Bianca sounded more disappointed than delighted when the Eversleys called her back to give her the good news.

'Unless you've changed your mind,' Pat said with more than a little hope in her voice. 'Or found someone else.'

'There is no one else,' Bianca said. 'Not at this late stage. That's why I had to call you.'

'Well *thank you*,' Pat said, her cheeks growing red with annoyance at Bianca's attitude.

'Yes,' Grace enthused, before her mum said something they might all regret. 'We'd be happy to step in.'

'But,' Hope cut in, 'as we're sure you appreciate, this is extremely last-minute and will mean we'll be working much longer days to fit everything in, so we'll have to charge you extra. And one of us will need to meet up with you today to get things started because we only have two weeks and two days until Christmas Eve, and the Mistletoe Dance is not a small event to organise.'

'I'm aware of the timing,' said Bianca. 'Charge whatever you must, I don't care. All that matters is that this damn thing goes ahead. Although if I had my way...' her voice trailed off, and then she added, 'the event would be far more select.'

Hope raised her brows, muted the call and said, 'And none of the villagers would be invited, including us.'

Grace frowned as she pushed Hope's fingers away from the mute button and returned the call to speakerphone.

'I'm available this morning, if that suits you. Unfortunately the rest of the team are busy with other events but I can take some notes and get the ball rolling. I'm assuming you'll want something similar to all the previous years, but perhaps this year we could change things up a little. I've got some ideas I'd like to discuss with you. Shall we say around ten-fifteen?'

Bianca gasped. 'Ten-fifteen? That's fifteen minutes from now!'

'I don't have far to come,' Grace said, grinning, 'and the sooner we get started, the better.'

The ornate iron gates of Betancourt were visible from the sitting room of The White

House, and Grace only had to cross the road to get there. Although the Eversleys were all still seated around the kitchen table, and their kitchen was at the rear of their cottage so they couldn't see the gates from there.

'Very well. Ten-fifteen it is.'

'We'll require a fifty per cent deposit today,' Hope announced, 'as it's such short notice. We treat all our clients equally, and can't make exceptions.'

Bianca's intake of breath was audible but she quickly recovered herself. 'That's not a problem. I assume you take cards?'

'That'll do nicely,' Hope confirmed. 'We'll email an invoice this morning, for immediate payment. What's your email?'

Bianca tutted before giving the details.

'Thank you for thinking of Eversley Events,' Simon said, with more than a hint of sarcasm in his voice.

'I didn't,' said Bianca. 'Calling you was my step son's idea. Please don't be late. I have a terribly busy day.'

Pat opened her mouth, no doubt with a sharp retort, but Bianca had already rung off.

'The bloody cheek of that woman!' Hope snapped. 'Call her back and tell her to bugger off and find someone else.'

'No!' Grace shrieked. 'And since when do we ask for a fifty per cent deposit?'

'Since Bianca Betancourt deigned to

29

honour us with her business,' Hope smirked, leaning back in her chair. 'She should be thanking us profusely for doing this for her. Not telling you not to be late.'

'We're not doing this for her,' Grace said. 'We're doing this for Russell ... and Archie and Griff.'

'We're doing this for Francesca,' said Pat, her voice tinged with sympathy as she took a deep breath. 'But I agree with Hope. A 'thank you' would've been nice.'

Simon nodded. 'I don't suppose those words are in her vocabulary. And we're also doing this for the village. Everyone looks forward to the Mistletoe Dance. Including us.'

Hope sniggered. 'Grace is doing this to get a date with Russell. And a kiss under the mistletoe.' She playfully nudged Grace's arm.

'What's wrong with that?' Grace said, already picturing the kiss. 'You did hear what Bianca said, didn't you? That her step son had suggested us.'

'I don't want to burst your bubble, sweetheart,' Simon said as he reached out and squeezed Grace's hand, 'but she does have two step sons.'

Grace snorted a derisive laugh. 'One of whom is finally falling in love with me but can't admit his feelings, and one of whom can hardly remember I exist. I think we all know which one of her step sons she meant. It was obviously Russell.'

'I think I agree with Grace,' Pat said. 'It was probably Russell. He has been far more attentive recently.'

'Yeah,' said Hope. 'Every time I turn around lately, Russell seems to pop up from nowhere. All joking aside, I think he's definitely going to ask you to be his date for the dance.'

'Are you sure you don't mind meeting Bianca on your own?' Pat asked. 'I can move a few things around and come with you, if you like.'

'I'll be fine, Mum. It's not the first time I've met a client on my own. We've all done it several times. And this isn't even a new client, really. We know Bianca.'

'That's precisely my point. We *do* know Bianca. I don't want her bullying you.'

'She won't bully me, Mum. I won't let her.'

'It was Grace who just bullied her,' Hope giggled. 'Did you hear how shocked she was when you suggested ten-fifteen?'

'Oh my God!' Grace leapt off her chair, knocking it to the floor and making Lady E, who had been curled up fast asleep in her basket beside the large green Aga, jump up and skitter back and forth for a second or two. 'I'd better not be late. It's five past ten already. Has anyone seen my handbag? And my iPad?' She frantically glanced around her.

'They're on the window seat where you left them earlier.' Hope pointed to the cushioned window seat where Grace had been sitting prior to taking Lady E for her walk.

'Thank you,' Grace said, grabbing the iPad and stuffing it into her large handbag. 'Love you all. See you later.'

She hurried from the kitchen into the hall and deposited her handbag on the hall table and then threw on her coat, scarf, gloves and bobble hat which were all still a little damp from the earlier soaking. This time Grace did take an umbrella. Betancourt might be just across the road but the drive leading to the front door of the impressive but understated, frontage of the stately home was a good half a mile long.

'Take your car,' Simon yelled.

'Don't you dare,' Hope countered. 'Think of the planet.'

'Think of catching pneumonia,' Pat cried out.

'I'm taking an umbrella,' Grace responded, tossing her handbag onto her shoulder, and closing the front door behind her.

She opened the umbrella and after a quick glance from left to right, dashed across

Folkestone Road. It was one of two main roads through the village and wound its way down the cliffside and into Folkestone. The other main road was London Road, but most of the traffic on this part of the coast travelled along the motorway, avoiding Betancourt Bay entirely.

The rain stopped the moment Grace shoved open one of the pair of ornate, black iron gates of Betancourt, and she virtually skipped along the sweeping curved drive, jumping puddles as she went.

The wide green lawns either side of the drive were mowed to perfection and looked immaculate even in December. The letter B – for Betancourt – was traced out, no doubt with great care, in the centre of each lawn. The only other greenery 33etweenn the gates and the house were the rows of shrubs and trees lining the walls surrounding the estate. They were apparently planted to conceal the stonework but Grace was not sure why. The warm sandy colour of the natural stone was beautiful. Though perhaps, looking out from the house and seeing high walls all around, each and every day, might make the occupants feel as if they were in a prison after a while. Albeit a somewhat luxurious one.

The last time Grace was at Betancourt was for the annual Summer Fayre. Russell had come home for that but not Griff. Most of the stalls were set up on the front lawns each year, but afternoon tea was taken in the beautiful gardens at the rear of the house which were always resplendent and brimming with colour.

The rear gardens were enclosed by the continuation of the shrubs and trees shielding the frontage. The lawns to the rear weren't as manicured as those to the front and were dotted here and there with more shrubs and trees. On each side sat a copse of trees and to the centre there was a formal knot garden, a rose garden – the bushes of which would now be pruned for the winter, a kitchen garden to the left and a wildflower garden to the right.

From a raised terrace running the width of the rear of the house, York stone steps led down to a broad path that zig-zagged to the left and right at various intervals, down the centre of the garden, as far as the eye could see, until it came to a large lake with a fountain almost as grand as the one on Lake Geneva.

Beyond the lake were the cliffs and below them, the sweep of Betancourt Bay, the sandy beach, and the sea. A pair of black, ornate iron gates, similar to those at the front, sat to one side of the garden at the edge of the cliff, and steps led down to the beach below.

The view from the garden was breathtaking and the view from the terrace and the house, more so. Locke Isle was clearly visible, but on a cloudless day, one could see far beyond the island and some days, even the coast of France was within sight.

The same vista could be seen from Lookout Point where, it could be argued, the view was even better as that sat on the highest part of the cliffs.

Grace loved looking out at Locke Isle, and she loved the stories and the legends about it. There was one story she loved above all others, mainly because it involved the Betancourts.

Legend had it that the Lockes and the Betancourts were once sworn enemies. Lord Locke, as that particular man was known, before he lost his title – and his head – to Queen Mary, or Bloody Mary as she was called by many, had three sons but only one daughter, Elizabeth. Much to his fury, she fell in love with a son of the then Baron Betancourt. But the two fathers hated each other and forbade the union.

Desperate and in love, Grifforde Betancourt, the Baron's eldest son, and the current Griff's namesake, took a boat to the island one dark night and Elizabeth Locke met him on the sands. They planned to return to the mainland and then to elope, but the weather turned suddenly, as it often did in this part of the English Channel, and when they were halfway across a storm swept in and gigantic waves cast the lovers into the bitterly cold sea.

Grifforde's younger brother happened to be on his way home from a night in a tavern in Folkestone with some friends and as they reached Lookout Point, they all heard Grifforde and Elizabeth call out to one another, or so they said. At the time they had no idea where the couple were but there was a full moon that night and one of them spotted the lovers floundering in the high seas. Grifforde and Elizabeth managed to find each other in the swell but the waves and currents were too strong for them. They clung to one another and kissed before the sea dragged them down to the depths and to their deaths.

It was a story Grace loved to hear, and one Granny Joy loved to tell.

'It's said that you can hear the lovers calling to one another when there are storms and the wind is in the right direction,' Granny Joy had told Grace.

Sadly, Grace had never heard them, despite often going to Lookout Point in stormy weather, just to see if she could.

There were other stories about

Betancourt, all of which Grace loved. She loved the place and always had. It was such a shame it was Griff who would inherit it and not Russell.

Although, to be fair to Griff, he had seemed to be the one who felt the same as she did about it growing up. Probably more so as it would go to him when Archie passed away. Russell hadn't really said how he felt about that, apart from once when he was about twelve and he'd told her that he was glad Griff was the eldest son.

'It's not like it was in the old days, of course,' he'd said. 'We don't own all the land we once did and we don't have all the responsibilities for the villagers and stuff like that, but being head of this family and the one in charge of Betancourt is still a huge task, and I'm glad it's Griff and not me who has to deal with it.'

'But where will you live when Griff takes over?' she had asked.

'It'll still be my home,' he had said. 'Although I'll probably have a place in London, like Dad has now. Both Griff and I will be working for the family firm after school and university, so I'll only come home for high days and holidays. It'll be Griff who spends most of his time here. I'll be pretty much care free and could live anywhere. Within reason. I wouldn't need to be at our

37

auction house in London on a daily basis.'

'Is it an actual house?' Grace had asked.

The only firm of auctioneers she'd ever visited were in Folkestone, the year before that conversation, and their offices were at the rear of a large warehouse, which was overflowing with furniture, toys, bric-a-brac, ornaments, jewellery, and more. Granny Joy had taken Grace with her to have an old vase she'd found in a boot sale valued. Granny Joy had paid fifty pence for it and It had subsequently sold at auction for two hundred pounds. But Grace had heard of much grander auctioneers, like Sotheby's and Christie's, and of course, Betancourt's.

Russell had smiled at her question and nodded. 'Our offices are in a former house, yes. A rather grand place in the heart of Mayfair.'

'And you sell anything and everything?'

'Not quite. We sell fine arts and antiques, mainly, but also books, wine, and jewellery.'

Grace couldn't imagine moving away from Betancourt Bay as a child, and even now the thought of living elsewhere never appealed to her. Eversley Events had been up and running for a year by the time she left school after passing several A levels, and although her parents encouraged her to go to university, all she wanted was to join the family business.

Unlike Hope, who couldn't wait to go to university. But she also returned once she'd got her degree, and joined Eversley Events, which by then was already a thriving business.

Grace arrived at the double front doors of Betancourt and took a deep breath before ringing the bell. She had told her mum that she was happy to meet Bianca on her own but in truth, the woman made her nervous and always had. There was something in the way Bianca looked at people, and it wasn't simply her look of distain. There was something almost predatory about her.

As Grace waited, she wished she had changed her clothes. She was still wearing the jeans and Christmas-themed jumper she had put on to take Lady E for her walk, and a berry-red jumper with a green Christmas tree decorated with tiny flashing lights, didn't exactly scream, professional, events planner.

She hadn't checked her hair either and it was clearly working itself loose from the French plait she had hastily tied after her seven-thirty a.m. shower, because several strands now tickled her nose and chin. She was trying to push them back into place when one of the double doors swept open and Grace gasped in surprise.

'It's you!'

'It is. And it's you.' Grifforde Betancourt's mouth curved into a smile. Not that sardonic smile Grace remembered so well, but a genuine smile, as if he was pleased to see her. And he didn't seem half as surprised as she was to see him. 'Hello, Grace. How are you?'

'What ... What are you doing here?' She wanted to add, and what have you done with the real Griff?

'Erm. I live here. From time to time.'

'I'm well aware of that. I meant, why aren't you in London?' Grace frowned. 'And why are you opening the front door?'

He raised both brows. 'I decided to come home early. As for opening the door, I find it helps people to gain access to the house.'

'Hilarious. Seriously, why?'

'You can't get the staff these days.'

Grace spotted Tabby Jenkins, the housekeeper, hurrying down the hall.

'I'm so sorry Mr Betancourt,' Tabby said as she approached.

He smiled kindly and somewhat sheepishly. 'Don't worry Tabby. It's not a problem. I'm perfectly capable of opening a door. And will you please call me Griff like you always have? Oh. And if you heard that stupid remark about staff, please forgive me. I was trying to be funny.'

'Is that what you were doing?' Grace said under her breath, although louder than she intended and Griff clearly heard it because he quirked a brow at her.

'That's quite all right, Mr ... Griff,' Tabby said, smiling up at him affectionately, and then turning to Grace. 'Good morning, Grace.'

Grace returned the friendly smile. 'Good morning, Tabby.'

Tabby had worked for the Betancourts for years but had retired two years earlier, until a couple of months ago, when the new housekeeper had a difference of opinion with Bianca and had walked out. Russell had told Grace about it at the Bonfire party in November.

'Are you coming in?' Griff asked.

'I'm meeting Bianca,' Grace replied.

He grinned. 'Did she insist you conduct your business on the threshold?'

'Did you have knives for breakfast?' Grace borrowed one of Granny Joy's expressions.

He smirked. 'I had poached egg on toast. Knives weren't available.'

'Knives?' Tabby queried. 'Weren't there knives on the table at breakfast?'

'There were, Tabby,' Griff assured her. 'That was another little joke.'

Tabby gave them both a look that said

41

she had no idea what was happening. 'I see. Well, unless you need me, I'll go and make some coffee. Or would you prefer tea, Grace?'

'Coffee please,' Grace said, relaxing a little as she finally stepped into Betancourt's spacious Great Hall.

Griff met Grace's eye and they surprisingly shared a smile. Only then did Grace allow herself to look at him properly. She soon wished she hadn't.

No man had a right to look that good in jeans and a Christmas jumper. Especially one with a huddle of penguins dancing on the ice amongst towering icebergs, beneath the Northern Lights. Although it did make her feel a little less self-conscious of her own attire.

'May I take your coat?' Griff asked, as Tabby hurried off in the direction of the kitchen.

'Don't you have one of your own?' Grace teased, now enjoying the banter between them, as was Griff if the smile on his generous mouth was anything to go by.

'Not as nice as this one,' he said, helping her out of her lime green coat.

'It matches your eyes,' Grace quipped, eager to hear what he would say next, but Bianca's voice cut in on them.

'You're here. Where's Jenkins?'

'*Tabby* is making coffee,' Griff said,

emphasising the name. His tone was much cooler than before.

'Good morning again,' Grace said, feeling as if she and Griff were naughty children about to be scolded.

Bianca looked as if she had just stepped out of the pages of a fashion magazine. She was immaculate from head to toe and not a single hair was out of place.

'Let's go into the morning room,' Bianca said, her expression making it obvious that she did not approve of Grace's attire.

'I didn't have time to change,' Grace said. 'I'd just returned from walking Lady E.'

'Fascinating,' said Bianca, sounding anything but, and then she glared at Griff. 'Are you joining us? It was your idea to call them, after all.'

Grace couldn't stop the gasp of surprise escaping as her eyes shot to Griff's face, and Bianca turned and flounced into the morning room which was to the left of the hall and the second door on the right.

'It was *you* who suggested us?'

He shrugged nonchalantly. 'It seemed to make sense. Your family organises events. We have an event that needs organising.'

'Oh. I thought... Never mind.' She smiled wanly, unable to completely hide her disappointment that it was Griff and not Russell who had suggested Eversley Events.

'You don't seem entirely happy about it.' Now he was frowning. 'Did I make a mistake?'

'No! No, it's fine. Thank you for thinking of us.'

'I often think of you.' He coughed and then ran a hand through his unruly hair which, like Grace's plait, seemed to want to go wild.

Grace wasn't sure what he had meant by that remark and decided it was better not to ask.

'I haven't got all day!' Bianca's voice boomed out.

'After you,' Griff said, indicating Grace should go before him.

'Are you being polite? Or are you sending me into the lion's den first? Oh gosh! Sorry. I was forgetting she's your mum.'

'She's not,' Griff said, tensing visibly and his voice was suddenly cold.

'Of course not. Sorry. I ... I think I'm having one of those days. I meant to say your step mum.'

Griff's tone and stance softened. 'Don't worry about it, Grace. We'd better get in there before Bianca has an apoplexy.'

Grace had been in the morning room a few times over the years, yet she still marvelled at its beauty. Now that the rain had stopped, the sun was breaking through the clouds and rays of sunlight filtered through the branches of a few tall trees set close to this side of the house and danced on the pale lemon and white walls. The furniture was mainly antique, made from yew and elm wood, but there was a modern and exceedingly expensive looking pale lemon sofa and two matching chairs placed in front of, and either side of, the large and intricately carved white marble mantlepiece.

Although the room was stunning, Grace realised something was missing.

'Isn't this room decorated?' she asked, taking the seat on the sofa that Bianca had pointed her towards.

'What's wrong with the décor?' Bianca's voice was raised in astonishment as she sat bolt upright in her armchair.

'I meant Christmas decorations,' Grace said. 'The décor is beautiful, but it's only just over two weeks till Christmas.'

'Isn't that why you're here?'

Bianca glowered at her, and a furrow formed between Griff's brows as he sat at the other end of the long sofa.

'Oh. I thought we were organising the Mistletoe Dance and dressing the Great Hall and the dining room for that. Are you saying there are other rooms we need to decorate?'

The Great Hall was where the actual dance was held and the refreshments were served in the dining room, both of which were exceptionally large with high ceilings.

'Of course there are!' Bianca narrowed her eyes and stared at Griff. 'I think this was a mistake.'

'I think perhaps we haven't explained what was required,' Griff said, meeting Bianca's cold stare, before looking directly at Grace. 'For several years, Betancourt has been decorated for Christmas by the company that organised the Mistletoe Dance. We haven't hung our own decorations since ... the Christmas before Mum died.'

Grace gasped in horror. 'You ... you mean you want us to do it all? Everything? From the lights on the outside to the stockings hanging on the fireplaces?'

'We don't have stockings hanging on fireplaces.' Bianca curled her lip in distaste. 'But yes of course. Everything. I thought I'd made that clear.'

'Erm. No.' Grace remembered that she hadn't been present during Bianca's call. Perhaps Bianca had told the others this teensy-weensy nightmarish problem and they had failed to pass on the monumental news to Grace.

'Are you telling us you can't do that? Are you wasting our time?'

'Bianca!' Griff snapped. 'There is no

need to be rude.'

'No! Of course we can do it.' Grace tried to stifle her rising panic. 'It simply means we'll need to rethink the timings. And we'll require more help. This isn't just an event you're asking us to organise. It's also the festive staging of a stately home. And that takes time, and a mountain of decorations, and a lot of pairs of hands. It's only two weeks till Christmas and it's our busiest time of year.'

'So you keep saying,' said Bianca, getting to her feet. 'I knew this was way beyond you.'

'It is *not way beyond us*.' Grace stood too. 'But we are a local business with limited manpower and only so much stock, most of which is already set aside for our regular clients. We'll need to hire help. We'll need to purchase or hire more decorations. And that will increase the cost substantially. But frankly, Bianca, it's either us, or you do it yourselves. That's entirely up to you.'

Grace was shaking, mainly with shock but partly with anger as she and Bianca glared at one another and Griff got to his feet and towered over both of them, but his tone was calm and collected.

'We're happy for you to do anything you need to in order to get this done, Grace, no matter what the cost. We realise we're asking for a minor miracle but the Mistletoe Dance is important, not just to me and my family, but to the village. We really need your help. As for manpower, hire however many people you require. We have a small staff here who would be keen to assist, I'm sure. And I'm here, ready, willing, and able. Just tell me what you want me to do, and I'll do it. Russell will be home next week, or perhaps sooner if necessary.'

Grace brightened at that prospect. And the offer of Griff being "ready, willing, and able" was conjuring all sorts of images in Grace's mind. Some of which she found surprising, and her cheeks warmed at the thoughts dancing around in her head.

She coughed to clear her throat. 'I'll need to discuss it with my fam ...the rest of the Eversley Events team, and get back to you.'

'Get back to us?' Bianca shrieked. 'You must start today, or it'll never be finished in time! '

'Bianca!' Griff snapped.

'Fine. You deal with it. This was your idea. I have places to be and people waiting.' She strode out of the room and slammed the door behind her.

'That went well,' said Griff, raising both brows as a sarcastic grin curved on his lips.

'I'm sorry,' Grace said, turning to face him. 'I really had no idea what was required.'

'It's not your fault, it's mine. No.

Actually, it's Bianca's. If she treated people with decency and respect instead of being so demanding, and insulting them, the company she has used each year would be here now, working.' He smiled suddenly. 'But I'm glad they're not. It's high time your family took over and organised the Mistletoe Dance. I know you'll do a good job and I can't wait to see what you come up with.'

'Really? Are you sure?'

'Absolutely. Aren't you?'

'Of course I am. But...'

'But what?'

She looked him in the eye and her heart skipped a beat. 'I ... I'm a little surprised, to be honest. Why the sudden change of heart?'

'Change of heart?' His Adam's apple rose and fell and he ran a hand through his hair. 'I haven't had a change of heart, Grace.'

'Oh come on, Griff. For years all you could manage to do was scowl whenever you saw me. The last few years you've given me that sardonic smile, and a grunt for a greeting. Now you ... you're saying you have faith in me and you can't wait to see my ideas? This isn't ... one of your pranks, like in the old days, is it? You really do want us to organise the dance, don't you?'

His mouth fell open, and he stared at her for a second. 'A prank? Is that what you think? I'm thirty-six-years-old, Grace. I don't do pranks. And certainly not when there's something as important as the Mistletoe Dance involved. I apologise if I've been rude in the past. That wasn't my intention.' He looked thoughtful for a moment. 'Or maybe it was. This may sound crazy, and it's not an excuse, but Mum's death affected me more than I realised and it's taken years for me to come to terms with it. I can't believe it's been twenty years. I still miss her, even now. Especially at this time of year. Sorry. That sounds lame. Have I changed?' He shrugged. 'Perhaps. But this is the real me, Grace. What you see is what you get.'

'The coffee's here,' Tabby said, as the door to the morning room burst open. 'Sorry for the delay. One of the chickens found its way into the kitchen and it took three of us to catch it and put it safely back in the coop.' Tabby carried the tray towards the coffee table and Griff stepped forward and took it from her.

'Chickens?' Grace queried.

'Don't ask,' said Griff, grinning.

'Really?'

Griff laughed and shook his head, placing the tray onto the table in front of the fire. 'Dad has decided to ... take up some new hobbies.'

'Ah.'

'Oh. Where is Mrs Betancourt?' Tabby

asked.

'She had somewhere else to be,' Griff said.

'I'm so sorry, Tabby,' said Grace. 'But I need to go too. I hadn't realised quite what was expected and I've got to talk this over with my family.'

'Can't you stay for coffee?' Griff looked as if he cared.

Grace shook her head. 'I can't. Mum, Dad and Hope are off to another event in about twenty minutes so I need to catch them before they leave.'

'Just us for coffee then, Tabby,' Griff said. 'I'll show you out, Grace.'

'No need. I can find the way.'

He grinned mischievously. 'I'm sure you can, but I want to make certain you don't steal the silver. Oh. That was a joke. Probably a bad one. Sorry. Please don't be upset.'

Grace grinned in response to his obvious discomfort. 'Damn. And I was so hoping to pop that rather large and lovely chandelier hanging in the Great Hall, into my handbag.'

He burst out laughing, and even Tabby sniggered.

'Good luck with that,' Griff said. 'I happen to know for a fact that it takes at least six men to lift it.'

'Or one incredibly fit woman, perhaps?'

The look in his eyes as his gaze swept

51

over her sent her nerve endings tingling and jingling, and she could almost hear the sound they might make. Much like the crystal droplets of the chandelier with six men lifting it, she supposed.

Three

Grace wasn't sure what had just happened.

Apart from organising the Mistletoe Dance, she had as good as agreed to decorate Betancourt inside and out for the festive season. And all in the space of two weeks and two days.

But that wasn't what was troubling her.

For most of her life she had only seen Griff Betancourt as a rather intense boy and then as an admittedly handsome man, but a man who was simply Russell's older brother.

Since the age of eight she had been in love with Russell. Every year she wished that she could be Russell's date for the Mistletoe Dance. Not once had she thought of being Griff's date. Never. Not even for a second. Apart from in those strange nightmares she sometimes had.

Russell Betancourt was the love of her life.

Russell Betancourt was her Destiny.

No man had ever made her change her mind about that.

She had dated about ten men since her teens but Russell had always been the one man she really wanted.

Why then, after all these years, and all the times in the past that she and Griff had been alone together, had her heart suddenly reacted to Grifforde Betancourt?

Why had it skipped several beats when he looked at her?

Why had she blushed at the thoughts dancing around in her head?

Why had she felt a warmth run through her when Griff had smiled at her?

Why had she enjoyed their banter so much?

Why, when she had said she had to go, had she actually wanted to stay?

And most important of all, why, when his gaze had swept over her, did she want to throw herself into his arms?

This was ridiculous.

This was crazy.

This was madness.

This was shock. That's what it was. This had nothing to do with how she felt or didn't feel about Griff. This was simply her panic, her confusion, her self-doubt all getting mixed together and making her think things she would never think on a normal day.

And it was because Griff himself had been so different today. Why was that, exactly?

Instead of the sarcastic and sardonic teenager, and the stand-offish and distant man, he was warm, welcoming, fun-loving, and friendly. A bit like he had been when they were young.

He had said that it had taken him years to get over Francesca's death, but Grace somehow knew that her death wasn't the only reason for the way he had behaved, all those years. There was something else behind his actions, she was sure of that. Had something happened recently to cause this change in him?

He had said he had never intended to be rude, but that's precisely what he had been, until today.

If Grace had believed in alien abduction and replacement with replicants, then that would've been her answer. But she didn't. And besides, Griff had looked and smelt far too good to ever be a humanoid.

Something had changed though. He had changed. What was it he had said?

"This is the real me, Grace. What you see is what you get." That too, had set her nerves jingling – but in a good way. In an exciting way. And Grace had liked what she had seen. She couldn't help but wonder what it might be like to 'get' Griff Betancourt.

A thought that concerned her far more than it should have as she hurried home to tell her parents of the task ahead. Not only were they organising the Mistletoe Dance, they were also decorating Betancourt in time for Christmas Eve.

Four

'You're back quickly?' Hope said, as Grace dashed into the kitchen, having thrown off her coat, hat and scarf, and tossed the umbrella to the floor in the hall. 'What happened?'

'I'm not entirely sure,' Grace replied honestly, now kicking off her boots. 'But I think we all need to sit down.'

'We're about to leave,' Pat said. 'Is everything all right, darling? You look rather flustered. Have you been running?'

Grace shook her head, pulled out a chair and dropped onto the seat. 'When Bianca first called you this morning, did she mention that, in addition to organising the Mistletoe Dance, she wants us to decorate Betancourt for the festive season?'

Hope, Pat and Simon all exchanged glances, and Pat pulled out a chair and sat down.

'No. Although I believe she did say

something about festive decorations,' Pat said.

Hope sat too. 'She said that we would be required to add festive decorations. I assumed she meant in and around the Great Hall and the dining room. I think we all did. Are you saying that she expects us to decorate the entire house for Christmas?'

Grace nodded. 'Yep. That's exactly what I'm saying.'

Now Simon sat and blew out a long breath. 'There is no way we can do that. There aren't enough hours in the day. Even if we had no other events at all, it would still be a mammoth task in the time left.'

'I know. That's what I told them.'

'Not to mention the fact that we don't have enough decorations,' said Pat.

'I know that too. But Griff said we can hire all the help we need and buy or hire all the decorations we don't have. Cost is no object. He even offered the staff at Betancourt's services. And he said he'd help as well!' Grace's voice was growing an octave higher with each sentence she spoke.

'Wait,' said Hope, her brows furrowed. 'Griff was there?'

Grace nodded again. 'Yes. And it gets worse.'

'How much worse can it possibly get?' asked Pat.

'It wasn't Russell who suggested us to Bianca. It was Griff.'

'Oh dear,' said Hope. 'Yes. I can see how you would think that was worse.'

Grace decided not to tell them the effect Griff's presence had had on her.

'Well?' she said. 'What are we going to do? I ... I've sort of agreed to it. But I did say it would cost far more than we had estimated. You haven't emailed the invoice yet have you?'

'No. I was going to,' said Hope, 'but minutes after you left, we had another surprise and we've all been trying to sort that out.'

'What was that? Not another new client? Because as much as I love the prospect of our business growing, I couldn't cope with more events right now.' Grace slumped back against the chair.

'Granny Joy is coming to stay,' Hope said.

'When? For Christmas Day and night, like last year? I know it was a bit of a disaster but I love Granny Joy.'

Last Christmas Granny Joy had stayed for one night. By the following morning she had emptied everyone's wallets after an evening of Poker and other card games, all of which she had won. She had told the same stories over and over and over. Drunk an entire bottle of champagne herself, and a bottle of white wine. Dressed Lady E as an elf, and posted several photos on Instagram and TikTok together with several videos of her and the family dancing to a selection of Christmas songs. Set fire to the curtains and not just the Christmas pudding. And on top of that, she had thought she was at home and had bolted the front door at midnight, forgetting Simon had taken the rubbish out. He was only wearing his Christmas PJs and it was snowing. After freezing for fifteen minutes and trying every door and window, he eventually resorted to waking Freddie Tollard who had just gone to bed, and borrowing the phone, to call Pat. Naturally, Freddie's daughter, Charlie had found it hilarious and had posted a photo of Simon in his PJs, on all her social media accounts.

'As do we all,' said Hope. 'But more so in small doses. Two or three weeks under the same roof might make me love her a little less.'

Grace tutted. 'You don't mean that.' And then she considered the matter for a few seconds, remembering everything that happened when Granny Joy had stayed over. 'Ah. Yes. I can see what you're saying. But we'll be prepared this time. Wait. Two or three weeks? Has something happened to her? She only lives a few minutes away, so why does she need to stay that long? Not that I mind.'

'She ... had a little accident in the kitchen,' Pat said.

'Like the one she had here?' Grace asked, concerned both for Granny Joy's safety and for the family.

'And then some,' said Hope. 'She has managed to flood the entire ground floor of her house.'

'Oh my God! Is she okay?'

'Apart from one singed eyebrow, yes, thankfully,' said Pat.

'Singed eyebrow? I thought Hope said it was a flood.'

'It was. But it happened last night and, although she was sensible enough not to turn on any lights as soon as she realised it was water, she lit a match and held it too close to her face.' Pat shook her head.

'Oh no!' Grace said, tutting. 'Why didn't she phone and tell us right away?'

'Because she was in shock, I suppose,' Pat said. 'She said she didn't want to wake us! I was so cross. She went to her neighbour's instead.'

'Ronald? The retired fireman?' Grace checked.

'Yes,' said Simon. 'He called out his mates at the fire station and they went and sorted things out. They wanted to take her to the hospital to get her checked out but you know your granny. She refused to budge.'

Pat tutted. 'And she told them not to call us because we'd only worry! She said she just needed a good night's sleep so she spent the night at Ronald's and phoned us when she got up. Which was just after you left.'

'Why does everyone call when I'm out?' Grace said, trying to make light of it all. 'So she's coming to stay with us today?'

'Your dad and I are going to get her now,' said Pat. 'Hope is sorting out the event today, so now that you're back, could you help with that? Or do you need to get back to the Betancourts?'

'They can wait,' Grace said. 'I'm more concerned about Granny.'

'It'll be fine,' said Simon. 'I'll just make sure we've got plenty of wine. And not just for Joy, but for us. I think we'll need it.'

'And I'll hide the cards,' said Hope. 'And all the matches.'

'I know it sounds funny but it's not really,' said Pat. 'I think Mum might have the beginnings of dementia. Perhaps I should have a word with her doctor.'

'Your mum has always been rather accident-prone,' said Simon. 'And she is in her eighties now. I'm sure it's nothing to worry about.'

'Say that when the house burns down

around us,' said Hope.

'Perhaps you're right,' Simon said. 'A quick chat with the doctor might put all our minds at rest.'

'I hope she's okay,' said Grace. 'The thought of her being unwell is pretty grim.'

'As your dad, says,' Pat said, squeezing Grace's hand. 'It's probably just Mum being Mum.'

'But what if it's not? Should I tell the Betancourts that we might be able to organise the Mistletoe Dance but we can't take on the festive decorating?'

'Yes,' said Pat. 'No wait. I think we must, mustn't we? We all know what Bianca's like. A bad review from the Betancourts is the last thing we need. We'll find a way to fit it in. If Griff said we can hire help, then that's what we'll do. I'm sure some of the villagers would be willing to lend a hand, especially if they were being paid. And there are always people looking for extra work at this time of year.' Pat sucked in a breath and puffed it out. 'Tell them we'll do it. Assuming we can get hold of more decorations and lights, that is.'

'Don't they have any of their own?' Hope queried. 'Surely they must have a few?'

Grace shrugged. 'I can ask. I know they did when Francesca was alive, but as Griff reminded me today, she's been gone for twenty years. Can you believe it's that long?'

Pat and Simon exchanged odd glances and Grace was about to ask why, but it had already been such a strange and confusing morning and what with the news about Granny Joy, Grace wasn't sure she wanted to know.

Five

Grace didn't have Griff's mobile number. But she did have Bianca's. The thought of speaking to her again today filled Grace with dread, so instead she tried to find the landline number for the house, only to find it was ex-directory.

She and Hope were with a regular client putting the finishing touches to a birthday party for his sixteen-year-old daughter, being held that night, so Grace didn't have time to mess around.

In desperation, she Googled Betancourt's auction house, and after the receptionist put her through to Griff's secretary, who in turn put her through to someone else, Grace found herself speaking to none other than Russell Betancourt.

'Grace? Is that you? Is something wrong?'

'Russell? Oh! Erm. I asked for Griff's mobile number.'

'So I've been told. He's at the house. What's going on, Grace?'

'Nothing's going on. We're just friends.'

'What? I don't understand.'

Grace realised he hadn't meant that question in the way she thought he had and she quickly laughed.

'That was a joke, Russell. Sorry. It's been one of those days. Erm. How are you?'

'I'm good, thanks. You?'

'I've been better. Look. I'm sorry to cut this short, because I'd love to chat. I really would. But I need to contact Griff about the Mistletoe Dance and the festive decorations.'

'He asked you then? He said he would.'

'Asked me what? To organise the dance and decorate your home? Yes. Well no. Bianca asked us. And then when I went to meet her to discuss it, Griff was there. Which was a complete surprise. He's changed. But that's neither here nor there. Erm. That's when Bianca sprung the news on me about decorating the house, and we almost came to blows ... Sorry! You don't want to know all this. I'm waffling. Wait. When did Griff tell you about this? I thought it all happened just this morning.'

'It happened last evening. The company we use called and told Dad that, due to an irreconcilable difference of opinion they found themselves unable to organise our event this year, or decorate our home. They said they wouldn't sue providing we reimbursed them and didn't give them a bad review.'

'What? This is news to me.'

'Ah. Bianca told you a different story, I assume.'

'A very different story. Wait. Why would the company threaten to sue? Surely it should be the other way around? You could sue for breach of contract. Russell? Are you still there?'

He coughed down the line. 'I'm here. Bianca can ... be difficult.'

'Tell me about it!'

'I'd rather not, if you don't mind.'

'Oh. I didn't mean, tell me about it. I meant, *Tell* me about it. You know. I was being facetious. Sorry. Not helpful. But then again. We are about to organise an event for you and decorate your house. I think, under the circumstances, perhaps I should ask about it, don't you?'

'When you put it like that, I suppose you're right. Please keep this between us though, Grace.'

'You have my word.'

He sighed loudly. 'Bianca and Dad are ... going through a rough patch right now and Bianca has been ... drinking more than she should, which sometimes makes her ...

volatile.'

'Blimey! I mean, I'm so sorry to hear that, Russell. It must be hard for you all.'

'It is. Unfortunately, she chose yesterday to ... drink rather a lot and she lost her temper and smashed several rather expensive decorations. We paid for the damages and for the company's discretion.'

'Oh my God, Russell! So Griff thought, why not get the Eversleys to step in and if Bianca does the same to them, who cares? No wonder he said money was no object. Thanks a lot. And I thought he'd changed! All he was doing was being charming so that I'd say yes!'

'No. That wasn't it at all, Grace. Griff suggested you and your family because he knows he can rely on you all, and if Bianca does ... go off the rails again, you'll keep it under wraps. But she won't. Not with Griff there. That's why he's home. Dad's not good with this sort of thing, so it's up to Griff, and to me I suppose, to make sure it all runs smoothly and the Mistletoe Dance is the success it's always been. Bianca wants to be involved and she wants to sort herself out. We are trying to be there for her and for Dad. Please help us, Grace. We really need some friends right now. The Mistletoe Dance was Mum's favourite event of the year. We can't bear the thought of cancelling it.'

Griff had said something similar. But this cast the event in an entirely different light. How could Grace and her family do their job, knowing that at any minute, Bianca might throw a tantrum?

'I don't know, Russell. We've got a few problems of our own right now. I'm not sure we want to work under that sort of cloud.'

'It's a lot to ask, I know, but we'll make it worth your while, Grace, and Bianca will behave. Griff has always had a way with her.'

'Griff has a way with all women.' Grace hadn't meant to say that out loud.

'He's definitely got the charm and the looks. But that's not what I meant. Bianca respects Griff. He knows how to handle her. I promise you, Grace. It'll be fine. And I'll come home soon, too.'

Grace sighed. 'You'd better give me Griff's number then. I'm not making any promises, Russell because this isn't just my decision. I'll have to discuss it with my family.'

For the third time today, Grace was tempted to add.

'Of course. I understand. How are they? Well, I hope. And talking of Hope, how is your sister?'

'We're all fine. Apart from Granny Joy. But that's another story. Text me Griff's number and I'll see what I can do. I must go.

Hope and I are working and this was meant to be a quick call. Erm. It is lovely to hear your voice though, Russell, and I look forward to seeing you soon.'

'Same here. Give my best to your parents. And to Hope. And thank you, Grace. I know you won't let us down. I'll text you Griff's number right now.'

True to his word, a text pinged through with Griff's mobile number seconds after Grace had rung off. Despite what she had told Russell about being busy, she dialled Griff right away.

'Griff? We need to talk.'

'Hello, Grace. This is a pleasant surprise.' He sounded genuinely pleased.

'It's not. I've just had an interesting conversation with Russell and I know the truth. I have to say, I'm not happy. Were you going to tell me? Or were you going to let me find out for myself?'

'Ah. I'm sorry. I was intending to tell you. I promise.'

'You would say that now, wouldn't you?'

'Let me explain.'

'I think Russell has done that. But I do want to set out a few ground rules if we're going to take on this job. Which I'm not saying we are. I need to tell my family about this latest bombshell.'

'Hardly a bombshell, Grace, surely?'

'That's easy for you to say as you're not in the firing line.'

'I wouldn't bet on that.'

'Whatever. I don't care. That's your problem, not mine. I'm at a party right now but I can meet you later.'

'Whenever and wherever you want is fine with me. I really am sorry, Grace. I made a mistake.'

'A big one. Meet me in the pub at eight.'

'The Royal Oak?'

'Is there another pub in the village?'

Grace heard his intake of breath and when he spoke, he sounded weary and oddly defeated.

'No. I'll be there.'

Six

Grace was still fuming when she broke the latest news to her family, and they had almost turned into the baying mob of Granny Joy's tales. It was all she could do to stop her mum and her dad from calling Griff and telling him exactly what they thought of such behaviour. Grace had told Hope about it at the party at which they were working, and it was Hope who had calmed the family down, that evening, oddly enough.

'But look at this from their point of view,' Hope said, once they were all seated around the kitchen table for their evening meal at six-thirty. 'Everyone knows Bianca is a bit of a Diva and we've seen her throw a tantrum more than once in the past, so it's not just down to drink. Unless she's always had a problem. Who knows? Anyway, they need, and want, the Mistletoe Dance to go ahead and so do we, and so does everyone in the village. If Griff can keep her under control, and from what you've now told us about your meeting earlier, it sounds as if he can, then it shouldn't be a problem. She isn't the first difficult client we've had and she won't be the last.'

'That's true,' said Pat, lowering her voice because her mum was asleep in an armchair beside the Aga and Lady E was curled up on her lap. 'But what with this business with Mum now, and all the events we've got booked, do we need to take on one that is definitely going to be a lot harder work than any of us expected?'

'But one where money is no object,' said Hope. 'I know I shouldn't go on about the money, but we really could charge a fortune, and they'd pay it. And we'd deserve every penny. And if Granny Joy does need special care in the future, that would certainly come in handy.'

'You're right about that,' said Simon. 'Although hopefully Granny will be fine.'

'Plus, they would feel obligated to give us a fantastic review,' added Hope. 'Especially after the things Russell told you.' She grinned at Grace.

'Some people might call that blackmail, Hope,' Grace said, pulling a face.

'I think you'll find it's called 'quid pro quo,' Hope said, grinning now. 'And it's an ancient and respected part of business.'

Pat let out one of her sighs. 'I'm not sure we have a choice. It's either us, or no one. We all want the Mistletoe Dance to go ahead, so I suppose we're in. Come what may.'

'Why can't Griff and Russell organise it themselves?' Simon asked. 'They're intelligent adults and they're both fit and healthy.'

'I think it's more about style, Dad,' said Grace. 'Yes, they could stick up decorations, and a tree, and get someone to do the catering, but would the Great Hall look magical? Would the dining room look inviting and the refreshments almost too good to eat? Would all the guests be talking about how wonderful it was for days and weeks and months afterwards? Probably not, I think.'

'I see your point.' Simon nodded. 'Well that's that then. I think we've talked ourselves into it.'

'I hope we don't live to regret it,' said Pat. 'Do you want one of us to come to the pub with you? I'd better stay here with Mum, but Dad could go. Or Hope.'

'Not unless you want to.'

'Not me,' said Hope. 'There's a series I want to watch on Netflix.'

Simon looked torn. 'Do you need me?'

'No. If I do I can call you.'

'Are you going to wash your hair?' asked

Hope.

'This isn't a date! Why would I do that?'

Hope shrugged. 'Because you've got pink goo in your hair from that party.'

Grace leapt to her feet and her hand shot to her hair. 'Why didn't you tell me?'

'I just did.'

Grace darted a look at the clock on the wall. It was encircled with so many twinkling lights she could hardly see the time.

'It's seven-thirty,' said Hope.

'I'm meeting him at eight!'

'Then you'd better get a move on. Good thing the pub is just next door.'

'Saints and sinners,' Granny Joy piped up and then quickly nodded off again.

It took Grace less than twenty-five minutes to shower and change and put on a swipe of lipstick and a dash of mascara. She wore a long, fitted black skirt, knee high black boots and a clingy, pale blue cashmere jumper and she stepped into a fine spray of her favourite perfume before heading back downstairs.

Hope grinned at her from the kitchen sink. 'I thought this wasn't a date?'

'It's not.' Grace's cheeks were burning. 'But that doesn't mean I can't look nice. Right. I'll go and give Griff the good news.'

'Is that all you're going to give him?'

'Oh shut up, Hope! This isn't a date!'

'So you keep saying. I didn't say it was. All I meant was I think you should give him a piece of your mind first,' said Hope. 'Make the man squirm.'

'Oh. I see. Yes. I'll do that. I won't be long.'

'We won't wait up,' teased Hope, laughing as Grace hurried towards the front door.

Grace took a deep breath before she opened it, as if building up her courage, and then she stepped outside and marched purposefully to the pub next door.

The Royal Oak was busy as it often was and it took Grace a moment or two to spot Griff. Her heart skipped a beat when she did.

He looked far better than he should have, and Grace had to remind herself that she was cross with him. He lounged in an armchair near the log fire staring into the flames, his long legs outstretched before him in a pair of smart and no doubt expensive trousers. One arm was resting on the table, the sleeves of his crisp white shirt rolled up to his elbow, while the other rested on the wooden arm of the chair and his agile hand fiddled idly with a button at the open neck of his shirt.

Grace couldn't comprehend the expression on his face but as she studied him from just inside the doorway, he suddenly looked up and met her eyes. The smile that stretched across his face sent tingles to parts of Grace that she had forgotten could react to such attention and the sparkle in his eyes danced as brightly as the flames of the fire.

To her surprise, he stood up, and as she walked towards him his gaze burned into her so intensely that she thought she might melt.

'Thanks for coming,' he said. 'Russell told me about your conversation and I wasn't sure you would.'

She bristled at his words, and as she took off her coat, she reminded herself that he had lied to her. Or tried to deceive her at least.

'I said I would. Unlike some people, I'm true to my word.' She draped her coat over the back of the seat he held out for her.

'Ouch. But I suppose I deserve that.' He bent his head close to her ear and the warmth of his breath sent shivers down her neck. 'You look beautiful by the way. What can I get you?'

For a second she was thrown off guard. Had he planned that?

'White wine, please. Large.'

He held her gaze for a moment longer than she would have liked and then he smiled the most gorgeous smile she had ever seen on him. He had this down to a fine art.

'Coming up.'

She took several deep and calming

breaths while he was at the bar and when he returned, she felt more in control of herself and her treacherous emotions.

'I really am sorry Grace. I know you probably don't believe me but I never intended any of this to happen.'

'Whatever. I've discussed it with my family and we'll organise the Mistletoe Dance and we'll decorate your house. But it's going to cost you. A lot. A huge amount in fact. And not just because of the time constraints, but because we feel we'll now be working in what might quickly turn into a hostile environment. If that's a problem for you, say so now.'

A frown formed and his lips pursed. 'A hostile environment? You make it sound as if Betancourt is in a war zone.'

'It may very well be so. Russell told me what Bianca did, Griff. And he told me the company could have sued you. That sounds pretty hostile to me.'

'You sound pretty hostile. But fine. I suppose you might have a right to be. Look. This all happened so fast. It probably shouldn't have but it took me by surprise. I should've been open and honest from the start. But to tell you the truth, Grace, I...' his eyes scanned her face and his cheeks reddened. He shook his head and ran a hand through his hair.

'You were saying?' She sat upright beneath his scrutiny.

His eyes locked with hers. 'I was saying, I hadn't seen you for a while and I was enjoying our banter. I suppose I was worried you might ... walk away if I told you the complete truth. But I didn't lie, Grace. And I was going to tell you. I was hoping you would stay for coffee and then, I would've had time to explain.'

'Easy to say that now.'

'Are you saying I'm lying now?'

'How can I tell?'

'Don't you trust me?'

'Absolutely not.'

His brows shot up. 'Why? Have I ever lied to you in the past? Have I ever done anything to hurt you?'

'Yes.'

He seemed shocked. 'When? What did I do?'

She leant forward and looked him in the eye. His Adam's apple rose and fell and she saw him swallow hard.

'I was fourteen, on my way home from school. You were sixteen and leaving the next day for boarding school. We met in the village and I tried to offer you some words of comfort about the loss of your mum. I told you how sorry I was and how much you and Russell would be missed. You gave me the coldest, cruellest smile I have ever seen and you said, "As if you care, Grace. I think we'll both be glad to see the back of one another." And then you walked away.'

His mouth fell open slowly as if he couldn't take it in and then he closed his eyes briefly and screwed up his nose and nodded.

'I remember that day. I'll admit I'd forgotten about it but now I remember. I can't believe you remember what I said, word for word. I had no idea. I'm truly, truly sorry. What you don't understand, Grace, is how I felt at the time. I ... I had just lost the most important person in my life, and I was convinced I was about to lose another. But we won't go there. The point is, I was lashing out. Not really at you but at myself. I was feeling sorry for myself. I was putting up a wall between myself and ... and anyone. Everyone. You. If I'd known I'd hurt you, I would've tried to make amends. I would've ... why did it hurt you? Why did you care?'

'Oh! Erm. Because we were friends. Or I thought we were.'

'But you believed you were in love with my brother. So why did you care what I said?'

Grace had just taken a sip of her wine and she spat it out at his words.

'What ... what did you just say?'

He quirked one brow and wiped a few splashes of the wine from his shirt with his fingers.

'I said, you thought you were in love with Russell, so why did you care what I said?'

'In love with Russell? What makes you say that?'

He frowned at her. 'I didn't say you *were* in love with Russell. I said you *believed* you were. There's a difference. Only from your tone and the expression on your face, am I correct in thinking that you still believe that? After all these years? Are you still infatuated with Russell?' The frown deepened.

'I'm not infatuated. Why does everyone say that?'

'Everyone?'

'Never mind. I don't know how we got onto this subject. We're not here to discuss Russell. Or me. Or even you. We're here to lay out some ground rules if my family are going to organise the Mistletoe Dance and decorate your house. Let's do that and then we can both go home.'

He still held her gaze and she looked away but was acutely aware that his eyes were still fixed on her.

How had he known about her being in love with Russell? Did Russell know? Would Griff now tell him?

'I promised Russell that I wouldn't repeat what he told me today. I want you to promise me that you won't repeat anything we say tonight. And I mean anything.'

He leant back in his chair and stared at her, his glass of beer hovering just below his mouth, his eyes intense, his jaw firm.

'You mean you want me to promise not to tell my brother that you've fancied yourself in love with him for more than twenty-five years, give or take a few years?'

'I ... I ... Yes. That's exactly what I want.'

The scowl of old had returned, along with the sardonic smile. 'You have my word. But I have to say, I'm astonished. I thought...' He shook his head. 'It doesn't matter what I thought. Let's discuss those ground rules and agree that we won't discuss this subject again.'

'That's fine with me. I understand that Bianca wants to be involved with the organisation for the Mistletoe Dance. We are prepared to agree to that but if she so much as raises her voice to any of us, we expect you to step in.'

'Agreed.'

'We will require carte blanche regarding purchases of decorations and anything else we need to achieve our task.'

'Will we have a say regarding those decorations? The style, for example? Or the colours?'

'I'm suggesting white, green, and silver. Are you happy with that? Do you need to ask

Bianca?'

His brows knit together. 'Just white, green, and silver?'

'Yes. I'm going with a Mistletoe theme. Mistletoe and silver bells to be precise.'

His eyes lit up for a moment and a small smile hovered on his mouth.

'Mum loved mistletoe, and silver bells.'

'I know. We're doing this because she loved them.'

'You are? Then yes. I'm happy. And no. I don't need to ask Bianca. I will tell her in the morning though. What about the tree?'

'Trees. We're having more than one. And yes. They'll be white, green, and silver too.'

'Trees? Don't we usually have one massive tree at the end of the Great Hall? A very brightly decorated tree.'

'You did. We won't. We'll have one massive tree together with two smaller trees and they'll be set up to look as if they are the entrance to a forest. There'll be snow at the bases of each. One will have white decorations, one silver, and one sparkly green. There will also be a tree in the dining room. That will have white, silver, and green decorations.'

'O-k-ay, I think.'

'We want to have a walkway of lights along the length of the drive, so there'll be white posts either side each draped with white nets of lights across the top and down the sides, creating a tunnel for guests to walk through. On the front door, there will be two huge wreaths, both hung with two silver bells in the centres. Is that a problem?'

'No. That sounds ... magical.'

'We'll hire the caterers we always use for large events. They're based in Folkestone and although they're fully booked, they're friends of ours and like us, will hire extra staff. For which you'll pay handsomely. Yes?'

'Yes. Are they good? Forget I asked. I trust you.'

'You do? Erm. They're good. But I'll take you to the restaurant they own in the town centre, for a tasting.'

He raised his brows. 'You're taking me out to dinner?'

'No. I'm taking you for a tasting. You're paying.'

'Fine.' He jumped to his feet. 'More wine?'

'Yes please. No! Oh, okay. Just one.'

'Well, I am wearing quite a bit of your first glass,' he quipped.

'We had agreed not to discuss that.'

'Sorry. I was forgetting myself.'

He walked to the bar but he glanced back and smiled and for a moment Grace forgot just how cross she still was with him. Especially because he knew she was still in love with Russell and he had clearly thought she might be a little crazy because of that. The smile had gone when he returned.

'Are there any foods any of you are allergic to? We'll have the food laid out in large shallow boxes designed especially for the event. They'll look like presents and there'll be cards attached that look like gift cards, only they'll say what's in the food, so that people with peanut allergies, or shell fish allergies, etc. will know exactly what they can and can't eat.'

'None of us have allergies, but I can't abide the taste of anchovies. I know that's weird, but there it is.'

'I'll make sure all your food has anchovies in then.'

Grace tried to retain a straight face, but her lips twitched and he grinned.

'Thanks. At least you didn't say poison.'

'Now there's an idea.'

He reached out and poked her in the side with his finger. It was a friendly, silly gesture and was so gentle that Grace hardly felt it – but she did, and shock waves of delight bounced around her body.

'I have to go,' she said.

'But you haven't touched your wine, and we haven't finished.' Disappointment was etched across his face.

She knocked back the contents of her

glass in several gulps.

'My gran is staying with us because she flooded her house, and thanks to this and all our other clients, Mum is running ragged. I only said I'd be gone for half an hour and I've just realised it's later than I thought.' She stood up to leave. 'I can email you the rest.'

'When do you intend to start? Will I see you tomorrow?'

'I ... I'm not sure. I'll let you know.'

'Call me? You have my number now.'

'You're so right. I definitely have your number. Thanks for the wine. Good night.'

She grabbed her coat and threw it on and then she hurried to the door. Once outside she took several deep breaths and tried to calm her wildly beating heart.

'For someone who is supposed to be in love with that man's brother, you're making a complete fool of yourself over Grifforde bloody Betancourt, Grace Eversley,' she chastised herself.

'Grace?'

She almost stumbled as Griff said her name.

'What?'

'We are still friends, aren't we? I ... I haven't blown it completely, have I?'

'Erm. We're as friendly as we were,' she said.

'Hmm. I'm not sure what that means but

I'll take it for now. Let me walk you home.'

She snorted a laugh. 'I live there, in case you've forgotten.' She pointed to next door.

'I haven't forgotten. But statistics show that people are often attacked outside their homes.'

'Well that's a cheery thought. Thanks for that.'

They walked the few steps in silence and he stood behind her as she opened the pink front door.

'I'm glad your parents have retained the pink all these years,' he said.

'Me too. Well, good night once again. Thanks for walking me home. Get home safely.'

'Pleasant dreams, Grace.'

'You too.'

'Grace?'

'Yes.' She held the door open.

'In spite of everything, I enjoyed today.'

'I ... I did too.'

She stepped inside, closed the door behind her and leant against it.

Hope popped her head out from the sitting room. 'So if it wasn't a date, why did he walk you home?'

Seven

'Have you got the list?' Pat asked, as soon as Grace came down to breakfast the following morning.

'Yes. And I've checked it twice.' Grace laughed as she sat at the kitchen table and waggled her iPad. 'I'll send it to Griff this morning, and as soon as I've got his agreement to everything on it, along with Bianca's of course, I'll put it in our shared Betancourt folder. There's a subfolder called Mistletoe Dance, and one called House Decorations.'

'That sounds perfect. Dad is dealing with the office party in Folkestone today for Bishop estate agents,' Pat said. 'I'll need to stay here with Mum, so Hope will be taking my place at Kelly David's hen party.'

'Where is Hope?'

'Walking Lady E. She said you might want to sleep in this morning. You weren't late last night though, were you?'

Grace shook her head, her cheeks flushing at the memory of the previous evening.

'No. But I was exhausted. Yesterday was one heck of a day.'

'You can say that again.' Pat tutted. 'But it wasn't all bad. I've made an appointment to see Mum's doctor this afternoon, so hopefully we'll get some news on that score. Fingers crossed it won't be anything serious, just old age and forgetfulness.'

'I'll keep everything crossed. Do you want me to continue working on the event for the undertakers' Christmas bash? Or is there something else that needs to take priority?'

'I think the Betancourts, their decorations, and the Mistletoe Dance should take priority, don't you?'

Grace was hoping not to have to see Griff today. Last night she had the strangest dreams and she still hadn't got her feelings and emotions entirely under control. She was adamant that she was still in love with Russell, and yet she couldn't stop thinking about Griff.

'I could do the hen party, and Hope could deal with the Betancourts today, if you like. I know Kelly better than Hope does, so it sort of makes sense.'

Pat stopped stacking the dishwasher and turned and faced Grace. 'Is there something you're not telling me, Grace?'

'No.' Grace let out a sigh. 'Maybe. Griff knows I'm in love with Russell.'

'Good heavens. How do you know that?'

'Because he told me in the pub last night. Well, what he actually said was that I believed myself to be in love with Russell.'

'Just like that? What were you talking about?'

'This and that. We were discussing the ground rules for us organising the Mistletoe Dance, and then somehow we started talking about the past, and then if Griff had ever hurt me, and I told him about an occasion when he had, and that's when he said it. He said that he didn't think I would care about anything he said to me, because I believed I was in love with Russell, or something like that.'

'And what did you say?'

'I said that I wouldn't repeat what Russell had told me about Bianca, if Griff promised not to tell Russell about our conversation last night.'

'So you basically confirmed to Griff that you are in love with his brother?'

'Well, yes. I had no choice. I am in love with Russell. Griff did say he was surprised, although I think the word he used was astonished. And annoyingly, he said it was infatuation, not love, just like Granny Joy.'

'Are you so sure it's not? Are you certain it isn't just a habit? You were only eight, after all, when you convinced yourself that you had met the love of your life. You were both children, Grace. Has Russell grown into the man you thought he would?'

'Yes! I think so. It's difficult to say for certain because I haven't seen him that often.'

'My point precisely. You think you're in love with a man you don't really know.'

'People fall in love with people they don't know, all the time. It's called love at first sight.'

'Yes. But they are adults. All I'm saying is, keep an open mind. Before I met your father, I had convinced myself I had fallen in love twice. Both times I was convinced I had found The One. And then I met your father and I knew. The feelings I had for him were entirely different to my previous feelings. He only had to look at me and I felt as though my body was on fire. His touch, however slight, sent the wildest sensations running through me. And when he smiled at me, I almost melted on the spot.'

'That's how you felt about Dad?'

Pat nodded. 'And that's how I still feel about him. Do you feel that way about Russell?'

'Erm. I'm not sure.'

Grace didn't want to admit, either to herself or to her mum, that it wasn't Russell who made her feel that way, it was Griff.

'Then I think it's safe to say that my mum is possibly right. And so is Griff. It is infatuation. And infatuation is a very different thing from love.'

'Oh dear,' Hope said from the hall. 'Are we discussing Grace and Russell yet again?'

Lady E scampered into the kitchen and made a beeline for her water bowl. Hope followed and shook her head as she pulled out a chair.

'Why don't you just ask the man out yourself, Grace, and put us all out of our misery? Women are allowed to ask men these days, you know.'

'Hilarious. Maybe I shall.'

'Yeah right. Was that a pig I saw flying past the window?'

'Don't tease your sister,' Pat said. 'We were discussing the plans for today. Grace has offered to take Kelly's hen party if you'll go to Betancourt.'

'Forget it. Besides, Griff wants Grace, not me.'

'Griff doesn't want me!'

Hope grinned. 'I meant as the organiser of the Mistletoe Dance, Grace, not for his wife. Although…'

'Stop right there!'

'Your problem is you have no sense of humour.'

'Your problem is you have too much.'

'Don't bicker, darlings.'

'I'm off,' said Simon, popping his head around the door. 'What's going on here?'

'Not much,' said Pat. 'And considering how much there is to do, that's not good.'

'I'll get changed and get to Kelly's,' said Hope.

'I'll get the invoice for the deposit sent out to the Betancourts,' Pat said. 'Or you could take it when you go, Grace.'

'So I'm going to Betancourt, am I?'

Hope grinned. 'Well it is going to be your home one day so you may as well get used to it.' And then she darted into the hall and ran upstairs.

'I think I may pop into Folkestone and see if there are any white poinsettias in the market, or any of the florists. I think they would look great on all the small tables dotted around the dining room and perhaps one long row of them running the length of the dining table itself because that's where all the food will be laid out, as always.'

'I saw some last week,' Pat said, 'but I can't think where. The problem is, your dad is taking our car, and Hope needs hers to get to Kelly's, and I'll need one to get Mum and me to the doctors this afternoon, so I was hoping to borrow yours.'

'I'll be back by lunchtime.'

'Perfect. Then may I give you a list of things I need from town? But it will mean dashing around a bit.'

'That's fine. I'll keep a look out for decorations while I'm there. You never know. I might find something wonderful.'

Grace was glad of the excuse to spend the morning in town. Now she would at least be telling the truth if Griff or Bianca asked where she was all morning. She could honestly say she was running errands for her mum.

And the sooner she headed out the better.

It felt colder today than it had yesterday but thankfully, although the clouds were threatening rain, so far it was dry. The last thing she wanted was to have to carry an umbrella around town, especially if she was going to have her hands full with shopping.

As she climbed into her car, she cast a glance at the gates of Betancourt and couldn't stop her gaze from travelling up the drive. The double doors were shut tight and there was no sign of any of the occupants being out and about. She pushed the start button, gunned the engine and drove down Folkestone Road towards the town itself.

She parked in the Harbour Arm car park

first. Her mum wanted a jar of honey from one of the stalls in the Marketplace, and Grace wanted to check out some of the other stalls there and also in The Goods Yard and on the Harbour Arm itself. At this time of year there was a Christmas Market which increased the number of stalls in and around the area by at least twice the amount.

She found several rolls of wide, white ribbon on one stall, perfect for making bows, tying things to the trees, and various other uses. She found some white and green cards, ideal for the gift tags she had told Griff about last night.

There were even some small white poinsettia plants on another stall, potted, as it so happened, in little silver pots. She could tie a green sparkly ribbon around each pot and have those dotted between the larger plants she was hoping to find. If she could have those in green pots and find some silver ribbon to match the green ribbon, that would look stunning on the tables. It wasn't long before she spotted exactly what she wanted.

And it wasn't long before she also spotted Griff. Not that spotted was the right word. She squeezed through a crowd of shoppers only to find herself staring at his chest. She didn't realise it was his chest until she heard his voice.

'This is a nice surprise.'

She raised her eyes to his. So much for avoiding him by coming into Folkestone.

'Yes. Isn't it? I wouldn't have thought a Christmas Market was exactly your thing.'

'Wouldn't you? Well there you'd be wrong. I love Christmas Markets. I love the variety of stalls, the smells, the food and drink, the unusual gifts, the people you can bump into. I was thinking of going for a mug of hot chocolate. Fancy joining me?'

She raised her brows. 'Hot chocolate? With cream and marshmallows?'

'Obviously.'

She scrunched up her face. 'I'd love to but … Mum's given me a list twice as long as Santa's and I need to get to the florist, the butcher, the baker and–'

'Don't tell me, let me guess. The candlestick maker?'

'What? Oh yes. Hilarious. No. But close. The chemist.'

'Or … I could treat you to a glass of champagne at The Lighthouse Champagne Bar at the end of the Harbour Arm. Come on Grace. Five minutes, that's all.'

'Okay. You've twisted my … harbour arm.'

'Hmm. Don't give up the day job.'

He took her hand in his to lead her through the crowd, and as he did so, they shot a look at one another.

Had he felt that bolt of electricity too?

Grace blushed and averted her eyes. Griff coughed to clear his throat, but they still held hands as they wove their way towards the Harbour Arm.

The Lighthouse Champagne Bar was packed, but it seemed Griff knew one of the staff and before many minutes had passed, they were seated at a table holding a large glass of bubbly each and toasting to the preparations for the Mistletoe Dance to run smoothly.

'How is Bianca today?' Grace asked.

'In a good mood, surprisingly.'

'Mum is sending you the deposit invoice today, so that might not last.'

'I'll pay it before she sees it. Dad is taking her out for lunch, which could go either way.'

'It's none of my business, I know, but have they been having troubles for long?'

'Since the day after their wedding,' he said, and although Grace assumed he was being facetious, she wasn't entirely sure due to the serious expression on his face.

'They've been married for about sixteen years, haven't they?'

'Yep. Sixteen glorious years of Bianca living in our house. What a joy that's been. Sorry. That was mean.'

'You've never really liked her, have you?'

He shook his head. 'No. And that's partly

97

my fault. As I said yesterday, I was so upset about losing Mum. When Dad met and married Bianca I couldn't really believe it. Obviously, I didn't expect him to pine for Mum for eternity, but I did sort of hope he wouldn't rush into marriage with someone else. Even if he'd married a saint, I don't think I'd have been pleased though. I did try to get along with Bianca and I still do, but we're as different as chalk and cheese. I think we tolerate one another.'

'Your mum was a very special woman. She would be a hard act for anyone to follow.'

He smiled at her. 'She was. But it isn't just that. I do want Dad to be happy and I did want him to find love again. But...' he shot a look at her from beneath long dark lashes. 'He has a habit of choosing the wrong woman.'

'Oh? You make that sound as if there have been others?'

He held her gaze. 'There have. Or should I say, there has.'

That was a surprise. 'Really? Before Bianca?'

He shook his head. 'No. Before Mum.'

'Before Francesca!' That was an even bigger surprise.

He looked her directly in the eye. 'That's a surprise?'

Grace nodded.

Griff sighed. 'Then the less said about that the better.'

'You can't leave it at that! I mean, of course you can. It's your family. But anything you say is safe with me. And I've always been...'

'In love with my brother?'

'That wasn't what I was going to say. I was going to say, interested in your family.'

He remained silent and studied her face. 'Okay. Dad was in love with another woman. But, sadly, she wasn't in love with him. They dated for a while and then ... she met someone else and fell head over heels in love. She dumped Dad, and she married her new love a couple of years later. Dad married Mum on the rebound, a few months after the other woman dumped him, but not before he'd made a total fool of himself by begging the other woman to take him back. He was still in love with the other woman when he married Mum and Mum knew it.'

'Bloody hell! I had no idea.'

'Clearly. Neither did I until shortly before Mum died. I heard Dad tell her that although he had loved the other woman, for many years, he had grown to love Mum far more, and he had genuinely loved Mum when she died. He was totally heart broken. And yet again, he married someone on the rebound. Namely, Bianca. Although not as fast this time.'

'I'm so sorry, Griff. Did you ever find out who the other woman was?'

'Yes. I know who she is.'

'Oh?'

'That, I am *not* telling you, Grace. Sorry, but I'm not.'

'Okay. I don't suppose it's anyone I would know so it's none of my business. Not that it matters, but does Bianca know?'

He shrugged. 'No idea. But somehow, I think she might.'

'Mum told me today how she felt when she met Dad. We were ... discussing something about love, and she suddenly told me that she just knew she'd marry Dad because of the way he made her feel. They've been married for thirty-seven years and she said he still makes her feel the same as he did all those years ago. That's true love for you.'

'Yes. I suppose it is.'

'You don't believe in marriage, do you?'

'Don't I?'

'You've always said you don't. At least you've often said you won't marry.'

He shook his head. 'I've only said I won't marry the wrong woman. I've seen what marriage to the wrong person can do. I know Dad did love Mum, eventually, and they were definitely happy together. But Dad doesn't love Bianca, and I don't understand why he married her. Or why they don't get divorced. I'm determined never to make that mistake. Or as determined as I can be. I'm not sure we can choose whom we fall in love with, but we can choose whom we marry. Look at your parents for example. That's what a marriage should be like. That's the sort of marriage I want. One that will last a lifetime.'

'Wow. Who knew you were such a romantic?'

He met her gaze and held it. 'You have no idea, Grace. Believe me.'

'That's the sort of marriage I want too. Like Mum and Dad's. But the man I marry will have to love Christmas, because it's my favourite time of year.'

'I love Christmas. Not that I'm suggesting...' he shrugged.

'No. Of course not. I understand.'

'You love my brother. At least you think you do, so ...' he shrugged again.

'Yes. Exactly.'

'Erm. I hate to bring this up, Grace, but although Russell enjoys Christmas, it's not his favourite time of year. He's more of a summer guy.'

'Really? Well it's not a deal breaker. Christmas is about family and giving and sharing, so as long as the man I marry is into that, that's fine. It's not about expensive gifts or impressing people.'

'Like having a big dance in the hall of your house, you mean?'

'No! Not at all. I love the Mistletoe Dance. I think it embodies the very best of Christmas because it's for everybody and not just the rich and the landed and... I'll shut up.'

Griff smiled. 'When Mum was alive our Christmases were far more enjoyable. Now they are about expensive gifts and impressing people.'

'They don't have to be.'

'All the while Bianca is married to Dad, they do. I think we should change the subject.'

'I think I should be going. I hadn't realised the time and I promised Mum I'd be home before lunch. I've still got to get to the other shops.'

'You do realise you used a similar excuse to leave me last night, don't you?'

'I didn't!'

'You did. But never mind.'

'Well I'm not exactly leaving you. I'll be coming to Betancourt this afternoon.'

'You will? That's good. I'll walk you to your car.'

'No need. But you're going to anyway, aren't you?'

'Yes, Grace. I am.

Eight

Back in Betancourt Bay, and having had a successful morning shopping, Grace dropped the car at home and then popped in to Catkin Cottage, one of four cottages on Oak Street, the road that ran from the corner of Folkestone Road up towards Betancourt Bay Café and West Wood, and then dog-legged off to the left.

Hanna Shaw, an artist, lived in the cottage and Grace wanted to ask her to paint a backdrop for the Christmas trees in the Great Hall at Betancourt for the Mistletoe Dance.

Hanna had created such things for Eversley Events before and they had a good working relationship as well as a friendship, and although this would be a rush job. A very rushed job, in fact, Grace knew Hanna would be unlikely to turn the offer of work down.

Hanna was an exceptionally talented artist but had not had the benefit of classical training, and therefore many galleries gave her the cold shoulder despite her skills with a brush.

She sold her art at markets, online, and through word of mouth, but she also worked on commissions, like the one Grace was giving her.

'Of course I'll do it,' she said when Grace told her what she had in mind. 'It'll be tight, but we can make the deadline if I start by say, tomorrow. I bet you're excited aren't you, to finally be organising the Mistletoe Dance? I know it's been one of your dreams for as long as I've known you.'

'I am. But then again, I'm not. We're so busy right now and this is a big deal, obviously. Plus we're decorating the house, inside and out.'

'Blimey. That's a challenge and a half. If you need a hand with anything else, just give me a shout.'

'Well, now that you mention it,' Grace said, smiling, 'we are looking for people who would be willing to lend a hand in return for a decent hourly rate of course.'

'Count me in,' said Hanna. 'I can't wait to see what cracker Griff's pulled this year. Does he ever bring the same girl twice? I've heard, from Barbra Brimble that all his women have three things in common. They're always gorgeous. They always seem to be madly in love with him. They never get invited back. Is that true? You've known the brothers all their lives, haven't you?'

Grace didn't feel comfortable talking about Griff like this, although only a matter of days ago she would've happily done so. But now, somehow, it didn't seem right. As for Barbra Brimble, as nice as the woman was, she was a dreadful gossip. She and her husband, Bernard owned Brimble's B&B on the other side of the tiny village.

'He hasn't said he's bringing anyone to the dance this year. And as he's home already, I'm not sure he will.'

Grace hadn't actually asked him. And now she wondered if he would.

'Well, he could take me. And probably most of the women in the village,' Hanna said.

'Not me,' Grace said. 'I prefer Russell.' Even as she said it, she wasn't so sure now that it was true. 'I'd better go. Mum expecting me for lunch. I'll see you up at Betancourt tomorrow. I'll be there from around nine-thirty onwards. Erm. One word of advice. Try to stay out of Bianca's way. She's feeling a little frazzled by the fact that this is all so last minute.'

'What happened to the firm that does it every year?'

'Scheduling conflict, I believe. Or they

forgot to book it in. I'm not entirely sure.'

'Oh well. It's worked out well for you, hasn't it?'

'I think so. Ask me again on Christmas Eve.'

Grace laughed and said goodbye and made her way back to The White House for lunch.

'Why are we going to see the doctor?' Granny Joy was asking when Grace opened the front door. She and Pat were in the sitting room and the TV was blaring so Granny Joy was shouting above the noise.

'Because you flooded your house and singed your eyebrow, remember?' said Pat.

'Of course I remember. I'm not senile yet you know.'

'That's a matter for debate,' Hope whispered, as she came down the stairs and met Grace in the hall. 'Are you eavesdropping too?'

'As the whole of Betancourt Bay can probably hear Granny, it's hardly eavesdropping, is it?'

'I heard that, Grace,' yelled Granny Joy. 'I'm not deaf either.'

'You should've whispered,' said Hope, grinning.

'I'm not blind either, Hope. I can see you loitering on the stairs.'

'Have we just covered the three brass

monkeys?' Hope said. 'Deaf, dumb, and blind? Or not, in Granny's case.'

'That's the wrong context, I think,' Grace giggled. 'And isn't it the three wise monkeys?'

'Not in this house.'

'What are you two laughing about? You wait until you're in your eighties and see if you're still laughing then. Why are we going to see the doctor?' Granny Joy asked again, but this time added, 'Are you ill, Pat? You don't look well, I agree.'

'It's time for lunch, Mum,' said Pat, and both she and Granny Joy appeared in the doorway, Granny Joy grinning, and Pat looking as if she bore the burdens of the world on her shoulders.

'I'll make lunch,' Grace offered. 'You go and sit back down on the sofa. I'll call you when it's ready.'

'That's kind, darling, but I made a casserole. It's in the oven and it should be ready about now. But you can dish it up if you don't mind.'

'Is Dad coming home for lunch?'

'No. He'll be out all day. But he is meeting me at the doctor's later.'

'Why are we going to the doctor?' Granny Joy repeated.

'We're not, Mum,' Pat said. 'We're going to the kitchen for lunch.'

Nine

'I don't suppose your auction house sells flowers, does it? Or that you know anyone who does?'

'Good afternoon to you too, Grace,' Griff said, getting up from the armchair in which he'd been lounging, reading a book by the fire in the plush sitting room at Betancourt. 'What was the question? I was engrossed in my book and didn't hear it when you came in.' He glanced over her shoulder towards the Great Hall. 'Who let you in? I didn't hear the bell either.'

'Tabby. And I didn't ring it. She spotted me walking down the drive and opened the door before I reached it. I need more flowers. White poinsettias to be precise. Plants, not cut stems. I've tried everywhere in Folkestone and I've rung around to all our usual contacts. I can have red coming out of my ears, but white? No.'

'And I'm sure they would look very

attractive,' he said, grinning. 'White poinsettias. Plants not stems. I'll make some calls. How many are you after? And is there a size or dimension?'

'Do you think you might be able to get some? Seriously? Because I was half joking. Or maybe not. I'm desperate. My only other option is to go to the New Covent Garden flower market in London. It's not in Covent Garden, it's in Nine Elms, but that's irrelevant. I can't afford the time. And they might not have them. It's not a guarantee. The traffic's horrendous at this time of year. At any time of year in fact. Not to mention the weather. And it means an early start. Like, leaving here before three a.m. to get there for four. Or there's Columbia Road. That's a thrill if you haven't been to Bethnal Green before. But that's only on a Sunday and we have just the one left really because there's no way I can leave this to the last Sunday before Christmas.'

'I'd like to say I'm following this conversation but I'm really not. However, I do know a man who knows a man who can usually get me anything in the flower department. I've often used his services and he's never let me down.'

Grace narrowed her eyes at him. 'What have you often needed flowers for? Let me guess. To impress a woman?'

He grinned sheepishly. 'I wouldn't use the word impress. But yes, I've been known to give the odd gift of some rather spectacular blooms from time to time.'

'Why doesn't that surprise me?'

'I believe, as I may be able to assist you in this dilemma, that sarcasm might not be your wisest choice.' He sounded serious but the grin belied his words.

'And I believe, as this is actually *your* dilemma, not mine, being a smart-arse isn't *your* wisest choice.'

'Point taken. I'll make the calls.'

'Thank you. I'll text you the pot sizes I'm after.'

'You want pots too?'

'That's how plants are sized. Usually. And they come in pots. Unless your man who knows a man, digs them out of the earth.'

'Ah. They'll come with pots.'

'And if, by any chance those pots could be either silver, white or green, that would help immensely.'

'Perhaps you should give me a list of your requirements.'

'I'll text you.'

'Will you be here all day tomorrow?'

'I can be. I like to get out for some fresh air every day, but if you need me here, then I'll be here.'

'I've got an artist coming here tomorrow

after nine-ish. I just want to make sure that someone other than you know who is here with her.'

'An artist? Are we having portraits painted?'

'No. We're having a back drop.'

'A back drop? Like one finds on a stage? Or a photoshoot?'

'Yes. I'm having her paint a winter wonderland scene to sit behind the trees I told you about. Don't worry. She's super-talented and it won't be like a school play or anything. It'll be a trompe l'oeil. Her name's Hanna Shaw and she lives in–'

'Catkin Cottage,' he cut in. 'I know her. Well, I know her art. I've got a couple of her paintings on my bedroom wall.' He grinned suddenly and winked. 'Wanna come up and see them?'

Grace raised her brows at him. 'Tempting, but no.'

She didn't say just how tempting. Or that she might like to take him up on that offer one day, if he were actually serious. Which, of course, he wasn't.

'Do you have ladders?' she continued.

'In my bedroom? No.'

Grace tutted. 'Ladders so that we can reach to hang the decorations. Or preferably a scaffold tower for the Great Hall. That ceiling is exceedingly high.'

111

'I'll ask the staff.'

'If not we'll have to hire them. Not a problem because we use them frequently, but if you have some it will save time and money because like everything and everyone at this late stage, most things and people are already booked up.'

'Send me a text,' he grinned.

'Make your own notes. It'll be easier and quicker.'

'Are you always this bossy?'

'Is it a problem?'

'No.' He cocked his head to one side and said in an extremely sexy voice, 'I rather like it.'

'Don't be a jerk. I don't have time for you to practice your flirting.'

Griff snorted a laugh and gasped in mock horror. 'Practice my flirting? I don't need to practice, Grace, believe me.'

'Places to go, people to meet.' She turned and walked from the room.

She did believe him. The effect he was having on her was more than a little disconcerting, and he wasn't even trying to charm her. No wonder all those women he had brought to the Mistletoe Dances over the years always looked as if they were in love with him. They probably all were.

Griff had followed her out into the hall. 'Is everything running to schedule?'

'I believe so. I need to bring some decorations and bits and bobs here tomorrow. Will there be people to help unload them? I can get them all loaded at my end but Mum, Dad and Hope all need to be elsewhere tomorrow. Hanna's offered to help. You're paying her by the way.'

'Happily. Cash, I assume?'

'That may be how you pay for most of your women, Griff, but we professionals take cards. Wait. That didn't actually come out the way I meant it.' Grace laughed, as did Griff. 'And, she might prefer cash. Although naturally, we'll invoice you for all the additional spending on staff etc.'

'I've paid the invoice your mum sent today, by the way.'

'Thank you. Right. I must get on.'

'Need any help?'

'Weren't you going to make some calls about white poinsettias?' Grace threw him a reprimanding look.

'I was. I am.' He turned on his heel and walked towards the sitting room.

'No point in having a list of things to do if you then forget to look at it.'

'Yes, Mum.' He glanced back at her and winked.

Grace bit on her bottom lip and watched him stroll into the sitting room and then she let out a wistful sigh.

She had spent just two days with Griff, and she was already missing him simply because he'd gone into a different room. If she was like this after just two days, what would she be like by Christmas Eve?

Ten

Grace hadn't seen Bianca since that first day in the morning room when the woman had stormed off, and by the third day, Grace was starting to wonder where she was.

She had been tempted to ask Griff this morning if Bianca would be joining them but she knew how he felt about his step mum and it was probably a good thing the woman wasn't around.

Hanna Shaw arrived at Betancourt a few minutes after Grace and it had been Griff who had been there to greet her, not Bianca or his dad.

'I've done a rough draft of what I think you might like,' Hanna said, showing Grace and Griff a sketch she'd made.

'This is exactly what I was hoping for,' said Grace, thrilled that Hanna had managed to capture what was in Grace's mind's eye, almost to perfection.

'This is stunning,' said Griff, looking

genuinely pleased.

'Thank you,' Hanna said. 'Will Bianca want to see it before I get started?'

'No,' Griff said, without a moment's hesitation, but his smile wasn't quite as broad as it had been. 'Oh. I've got your white poinsettias, Grace. I meant to text you last night but ... something came up. They're being delivered next week. Is that okay? And I've got some silver pots, green pots and white pots. They'll be here the same day.'

'That is brilliant, Griff! You're a star. Thank you.'

The broad smile returned and he beamed at Grace. 'My pleasure. And I've checked my list this morning, like a good little helper.' He pulled a face. 'If my colleagues could see me now.' He laughed and shook his head.

'You're enjoying this aren't you?' Hanna said.

'To my astonishment, I am.' He shot a look at Grace. 'More than I imagined.'

'Well don't just stand there,' said Grace, blushing under the intensity of his gaze. 'Go and do something useful.'

He pointedly spun on his heels and marched away.

'Don't look now,' Hanna said, nudging Grace's arm, 'But I think someone may have a bloody great crush on someone.'

'Is it that obvious?' Grace's hand shot to her face and her cheeks flushed even redder. 'I thought I was in love with Russell. But now I'm not so sure. Griff makes me feel... Oh.' She coughed. 'You didn't mean me, did you?'

Hanna shook her head slowly and deliberately and the grin on her face grew wider. 'No. But now I'm even more intrigued. You thought you were in love with Russell, the younger brother? But now you're falling for Griff? This could be awkward.'

'You have no idea.'

'Does Russell know? Does Griff?'

Grace sighed wearily. 'The truth is, I've been in love with Russell for most of my life. Since I was about eight, and I'm thirty-four now.'

'Blimey! That's some crush.'

'Yes. I know. I'm nothing if not steadfast. Although, having said that, I thought it was love but others said it was infatuation. I'm not sure now. But I am sure that Griff makes my insides turn to jelly with just one look.'

'And I think I can safely say you have the same effect on him.'

'Me? Have an effect on Griff?' Grace laughed at the idea. 'No. You're wrong. I think he likes me, as a friend, but you've seen the women he dates. They're all breathtakingly beautiful. The sort of women you find at the most glamourous events. Not the sort of woman you find organising those events, with her hair tied into a loose bun and wearing scruffy jeans and a Christmas jumper.'

'Don't put yourself down, Grace. You're very pretty.'

'I'm not bad. But I'm no beauty.'

'Beauty is in the eye of the beholder. And Griff beholds beauty. You can see it in his eyes and in his smile.'

'No. Honestly, Hanna. You're wrong. Besides. He knows I love Russell. Well, he says I only think I love Russell and that I'm simply infatuated.'

'He knows? How? Did you tell him?'

'Yes. No. He told me. He says he's always known. But Russell doesn't. So please, please don't say anything to anyone.'

'I won't. But you need to sort out how you feel, Grace. Being in love, or thinking you're in love with two brothers is a recipe for disaster.'

'That's what my gran says. She says it'll end in tears. But she means Russell. She doesn't know how I feel about Griff because she's not really with it right now. And come to that. I don't know how I feel about Griff.'

'I thought this job was going to be a hoot but I had no idea how much of one.'

'I'm not finding it that funny. I'm feeling rather bemused.'

Hanna linked her arm through Grace's. 'Let's get some work done. I find that often helps. So what's wrong with your gran?'

'We're not sure. Mum thinks it could be the stat of dementia. They went to the doctor yesterday and he did some tests. We'll get the results next week. But he thinks it could simply be age-related forgetfulness. Or it could be a vitamin deficiency. Or it could be a mini stroke. Basically, he doesn't know.'

'I'm sorry Grace. Let's hope it's the vitamin deficiency. That's easily curable. If you need to talk, you know where to find me. I know you've got your family, but the offer's there.'

'Thanks. Griff said the same when Mum called me here after they left the doctor yesterday. It means a lot to know there are people who care.'

Which reminded Grace of Bianca.

'I just need to check on something,' she added. 'Can you start without me?'

'Sure. I won't need you for a couple of hours at least.'

Grace went in search of Griff, and found him on the phone in the sitting room. He held a finger in the air as she walked towards him so she remained silent until he rang off, leant back in his chair and sighed.

'That was fun. Do you need me?'

'Where's Bianca?'

'What?'

'I was wondering where she was because I haven't seen her since Friday.'

'She's locked in the basement.'

'What?' Grace gasped with shock. 'Oh. You're joking.'

'But you thought it might be true.' He narrowed his eyes at her. 'Do you think I'm the kind of man who locks women in basements, Grace?'

'Well...' she grinned. 'No, of course not. But I was concerned that something might have happened to her. You said she and your dad were having lunch. Did that go okay? Tell me if this is none of my business.'

'This is none of your business. But I'll tell you anyway.' He sucked in a long breath. 'The lunch did not go well. Dad, Russell and I had a conversation yesterday. A serious conversation. After which we suggested to Bianca that a week or two in a private facility might do her the world of good. She agreed and she left yesterday.'

'Really? Just like that? She left? Is she coming back?'

'Yes. Yes. And yes. Hopefully in time for the Mistletoe Dance.'

'Wow. There's a lot going on, isn't there? But why didn't you mention this yesterday? I told you about Granny Joy.'

'Which is why I didn't mention it. You

have enough to worry about right now without adding Bianca to that list. I'd appreciate it if you kept this between us. You can tell your family, of course, but please don't tell Hanna or anyone else.'

'What if someone asks why she isn't around?'

'Tell them to ask me and I'll make something up.'

'You'll lie?'

'Not exactly. But I'll avoid telling the truth.'

'Does Tabby know?'

'Of course. She's like family.'

'And the staff?'

He shook his head. 'Just Tabby. Oh. And you'll be pleased to hear that Russell is coming home this Friday. I was just speaking with him when you came in.'

Grace tensed under his gaze. 'Why would I be pleased?'

He frowned and then gave her that old sardonic smile. 'Because you love him, remember? Or you think you do. Anyway. He'll be here by late afternoon. So only four more days to wait.'

'I'm not some love-sick girl, Griff. I've waited far longer than a few days to see Russell. Not that I'm actually waiting for him. In fact, I think perhaps Granny Joy – and you – may have been right. Perhaps it is

… was … merely infatuation.'

He sat upright and looked her in the eye.

'Good. Because I like you, Grace. And believe it or not I care about you. I don't want to see you get hurt. I love my brother dearly, but … he may not live up to your high expectations of him.'

'I … I don't have high expectations of him. I'm not sure I expect anything of him.'

'You think you've been in love with him for years and suddenly, just like that, you decide it's infatuation? Are you sure that's how you feel? Or are you simply saying what you think others want to hear?'

'Honestly? I don't know. I said I'm not some love-sick girl, and yet I've been behaving like a teenager with a crush for years. It's time I grew up and became a woman.'

'From where I'm sitting, Grace. You are very much a woman. Take my word for that.'

The look in his eyes and the tensing of the muscles around his mouth, jaw and neck told her he was struggling to stay where he was. Did he want to come to her and take her in his arms? Or was this her fanciful imagination running away with her again?

'And from where I'm standing, Griff. You are very much a man.'

His sharp intake of breath thrilled her. Hanna was right. She did have an effect on him. But not as great as she would have liked. He remained seated.

'Now which one of us is practising flirting?'

'Not me,' she said, fluttering her eyelashes.

She was about to say more when Tabby knocked on the open door and popped her head around it.

'Sorry to disturb you, Griff, and Grace, but ... your girlfriend is here. She's waiting in the morning room.'

'Girlfriend?' Grace shrieked, horrified.

'Girlfriend?' Griff queried, looking confused.

'Davina?' Tabby prompted.

'Oh, Davina. Yes of course. I'll be right there, Tabby. Can you get her some coffee please? She takes it black.'

'Already have.' Tabby smiled and left them, throwing a sympathetic glance at Grace.

'Davina!' Grace hissed between gritted teeth. 'You are astonishing! You have so many women in your life that you can't even remember the name of your current girlfriend. I do love Russell. I don't know why I ever thought otherwise.'

She turned and raced from the room.

'Grace? Grace!'

She heard him call her but he didn't

come after her and when she did see him again, he was heading towards the morning room. And his girlfriend, Davina.

Eleven

Grace spent the rest of the day caught between tears pricking at her eyes and anger raging in her chest.

That bloody man had been playing with her. He knew exactly what he was doing and he enjoyed every minute of it.

How could she have been so stupid?

How could she have fallen for his games?

How had she thought herself in love with one man for over twenty-five years, and then in the space of two days, have fallen for his brother?

Because anyone who believes themselves to be in love with a man they hardly ever see must be delusional, mustn't they?

Hope never behaved like this and she was younger than Grace.

'Is it safe to come in?' Hope asked, knocking on Grace's bedroom door.

'I give no guarantees. But I could use the

company. I bet Mum and Dad think I should be certified, don't they?'

'No. Of course not. I'm the only one who thinks that.' Hope dropped onto Grace's bed and scooched up beside her. 'Seriously, Grace. No one thinks anything of the sort. You're just a little too much of a romantic for your own good, that's all. Has he called? Or texted?'

'Griff?'

'No. Father Christmas. Of course, Griff.'

Grace shook her head. 'Why would he? He's no doubt having sex with his girlfriend. The obviously gorgeous, Davina.' Grace sneered.

'I have to admit I'm as surprised as you must've been. He didn't mention a girlfriend, did he? And I swear we all thought ... Well, that doesn't matter now. You'll get over this, Grace. You will. And you'll be stronger for it.'

'What doesn't kill you makes you stronger, right?'

'Right,' said Hope. 'And in the meantime, there's ice cream. Bailey's flavoured tubs of the stuff. Come down and have some and we'll watch a weepy movie together. That way you can blame your red, bleary eyes on one of those, and not a certain man we won't mention.'

'Bailey's ice cream?'

Hope nodded.

'And Dad's been out and bought chocolate flakes.'

'Chocolate flakes and Bailey's ice cream? Why didn't you say so earlier?'

Grace's heart might be breaking but nothing could ever be so dire as to stop her from eating Bailey's ice cream and chocolate flakes.

Hope took her hand and they ran down the stairs together.

'We've made a space for you here,' said Pat, tapping the sofa cushion between herself and Granny Joy. 'I'll make some tea.'

'I told you it would end in tears,' said Granny Joy.

'Wrong brother,' said Grace, and she leant over and kissed her gran on the forehead.

'That's what I said.' Granny Joy clearly had more to say. 'Grifforde is the one for you, Grace. Mark my words. Not Russell.'

'You have no idea how wrong you are, Granny,' said Grace, her heart breaking just a little. 'Where's Dad?' she asked Hope.

'On the phone with a client.'

'I'm never wrong about the Betancourts.' Granny Joy slapped Grace's knee, but it was a gentle slap.

'Okay, Granny,' said Hope. 'I think Grace has heard enough about that family to last her a lifetime. I think we all have.'

'And to think those boys might've been your siblings. Except they wouldn't be here, would they? Not if Patty had married Archie.'

'What?'

Both Grace and Hope shot a look at one another and then at Granny Joy.

'What are you talking about, Granny?' Hope asked.

'Patty and Archie. They made a lovely couple. He adored her. Worshipped the ground she walked on. Followed her around like a love-sick puppy. Even after she dumped him for Simon. Begged her to take him back. Begged her to marry him. Wrote to her every day. Even after he married that ... what was her name?'

'Francesca?' Grace croaked.

'That's it! Francesca. Silly man. He shouldn't have married her when he still loved my Patty. But men don't think with their heads, do they? And then Francesca fell pregnant and that was that. No way Patty would take him back if it meant he would leave his wife and child. No way.'

'Mum!' Pat shrieked, returning to the sitting room and losing every ounce of colour from her cheeks.

'I think you have some explaining to do,' said Hope, glaring at Pat.

'Is it true, Mum?' Grace couldn't quite believe it.

'Oh, Mum,' Pat sighed at Granny Joy. 'I suppose we should've known that one day it would all come out.' She shook her head and sighed again. 'Yes. It's true. At least, if Mum has said that Archie Betancourt was in love with me, that is.'

'Does Dad know?' asked Hope.

'Of course he does. He lived through it with me. The phone calls. The letters. But Archie did grow to love Francesca, and eventually he realised I adored your dad and would never leave him. Archie and I only dated for about six months before I met and fell in love with Simon. Archie always felt more for me than I did for him. That's the way of things sometimes. But as I told you, Grace, I knew the moment I met your dad. That was it for me. No other man stood a chance.'

'So Archie stalked you?' Hope said. 'That rings a bell. How weird that the roles reversed.'

'If you're saying I stalked Russell,' said Grace, 'then ... Okay. Maybe I did. But I didn't send letters. Or make phone calls. Or anything in fact.'

'You didn't stalk anyone,' said Pat. 'But I must admit, your dad and I were worried for a time. It was like history repeating itself, only reversed, as Hope said. It gave us the creeps. But we thought it best to leave it be.'

129

'So that's why there was always that tension in the air when you and Dad and Archie and Francesca met?' said Grace. 'I knew I hadn't imagined it.'

'And is that the "difference of opinion" you told us about?' said Hope. 'And the reason the Betancourts wouldn't give us any business after you set up the events company?'

'That was the difference of opinion, yes.' Pat nodded, as Granny Joy let out a snore. 'And I assume also the reason they didn't give us business. Although Francesca passed away before then, so either Archie decided Bianca couldn't use us, or Bianca found out somehow and decided she didn't like me around her husband.'

'Griff knows about you!' shrieked Grace.

'What?' said Hope. 'How?'

'He told me he overheard a conversation between his dad and Francesca. But he didn't tell me the other woman was you, Mum.'

'I wasn't 'the other woman'! That sounds as if we had an affair and we didn't. It was over between me and Archie the moment I met your dad. Archie married before we did and they had Griff and Russell. I fell pregnant with you and Hope after they were born. You know that.'

'Why did you decide to buy a house directly opposite Archie's home?'

'Looking back, that might not have been our best idea. But I loved Betancourt Bay and so did Simon. There weren't many homes in our price range back then, and Folkestone was too expensive. When this one came on the market, well within our price bracket, we came to look at it more out of curiosity than anything else. The moment I saw it I knew though, and so did your dad. We decided to purchase and be damned, as the saying goes. And the thing is, we couldn't have been happier here. We might not have been so happy somewhere else.'

'Poor Francesca,' said Hope. 'How sad to know your husband loves another woman.

'Loved. Past tense. Because he did grow to love Francesca. And she was good for him. Strangely enough, they were happy too. I think Francesca simply accepted the fact and she knew how much I loved, and still do love, Simon. She knew I'd never have an affair with Archie. Keep your friends close and your enemies closer, perhaps?'

'That's that done and dusted. Time for ice cream.' Simon came in and glanced around the room. 'What's happened?'

'Granny Joy let the cat out of the bag about Mum and Archie,' Hope said.

'I thought she would one day. And?'

'And it's all good,' said Pat. 'Isn't it?'

'It is,' said Grace.

131

'Weird, but yes,' said Hope. 'Erm. Does Granny have any other little bombshells to share with us?'

'Absolutely not,' said Pat. 'Now what are we going to watch?'

Twelve

'I know this is all supposed to make me stronger,' Grace said, next morning at the usual breakfast-come-catch-up in the kitchen. 'But I honestly don't think I'm up to spending the day at Betancourt. Please let me switch with one of you.'

'You're the one with the vision for this event though, Grace,' Pat said. 'But we understand and yes, of course. You'll need to tell us exactly what you want and where you want it and maybe a diagram or two might help.'

'I was going to be taking up the decorations and lights today so it's mainly lifting, carrying, sorting and then hanging. I've done a couple of drawings though to show you where I think things should go. They're in our shared Betancourt folder. Hanna will be there working on the backdrop for the trees. Which reminds me. Have we heard when they'll arrive?'

'No. They said later this week, I think,' said Hope. 'I'll check again. I know the sizes you requested are few and far between so maybe there's a problem.'

'Perfect! This thing is turning into a nightmare.' Grace shook her head. 'I'll go and see if I can get the mistletoe I ordered from that farm the other side of Maidstone.'

'You take care, Grace,' said Granny Joy who had joined them at the kitchen table this morning. 'It's going to snow. I can feel it in my water.'

'Snow?' Hope laughed. 'No chance. Those are rain clouds.'

'Snow. Mark my words. And not just snow. A blizzard.'

'Google?' Grace asked the Home Hub. 'What's the weather for today in and around Betancourt Bay?'

'The weather today in and around Betancourt Bay is 1 degree and cloudy with possible wintry showers, some heavy, along with strong winds.'

'There, you see. Snow blizzards.' Granny Joy stuck out her chin. 'I'm staying in the warm.'

'Sleet at the worst,' said Hope.

'I'll see if your neighbour, Ronald would like to come round for coffee this morning, Mum,' said Pat. 'Then I can help at Betancourt.'

'I don't need a babysitter,' Granny Joy stuck out her tongue.

'Clearly,' said Hope, as Pat left the room to make the call. 'What do we say if you-know-who asks where you are, Grace?'

Grace swallowed her mouthful of coffee and shook her head. 'Just say I'm busy with another client. I don't think he'll ask. If he wanted to know, or if he cared how I felt, he would've called or texted yesterday. I'm sure he's having too much fun to worry about me.'

'All sorted,' said Pat, returning to the kitchen. Ronald will be here just after nine. He's happy to stay until after lunch so that means we'll have the entire morning at Betancourt.'

Grace couldn't stop the twinge of envy twisting in her stomach. 'I'll make a move then so I should be back in time for lunch. Then we can have a catch-up and see where we are and what needs doing next.'

'That sounds good to me,' said Simon. 'I hope we don't see Griff today, because I might have to give him a piece of my mind.'

'Please don't, Dad.' Grace gave him a wan smile. 'I'd rather we just all behaved as though none of us could care about him and his bloody girlfriend.'

'Grace is right,' said Hope. 'Best to ignore him as much as possible.'

Grace got up and placed her plate and

135

mug in the dishwasher. 'I'll see you all back here around one then. Have a good day.'

'You too, darling,' Pat said. 'Drive safely. I'm certain it won't snow, but make sure you've got a blanket in the car, just in case. And a shovel. And watch out for black ice. I know it's 1 degree but there was a frost last night, so there may be ice patches on the roads.'

'I'll take care. Bye all.'

Grace put on her long, leather boots and then grabbed her coat, scarf, hat and gloves and wrapped up warmly before heading out.

She stopped for a second and looked at the sky. Granny Joy had often been right before, in spite of what the forecast said, but it didn't look like snow was coming and there wasn't as much as a breeze, so a blizzard was unlikely.

She forgot about the blanket and hurried to the door to get out of the cold. Once inside, she waited for the heater to kick in before pressing the starter and driving off in the direction of London Road.

It meant she had to drive past the ornate iron gates of Betancourt and try as she might, she couldn't stop her eyes from drifting along the drive to the front door. But just like last time, the drive was empty and the door was closed.

She was so busy looking at the door of

the house that she almost missed the turning onto Oak Street. The car skidded as she yanked on the wheel, but she kept it under control and then turned again into London Road and drove towards the motorway.

She switched on the radio and sang along with all the old Christmas songs that always played on the radio year after year. She loved doing this and yet somehow everything to do with Christmas had lost its sparkle and joy since yesterday. What a difference a day makes?

She tried to tune into another station that wasn't playing Christmas songs, but it was like finding a needle in a haystack, two weeks before the Big Day.

Her windscreen was misting up so she turned the heater up and used the washer and wipers to clear the outside. The mist inside wasn't clearing and she could hardly see the road ahead and then she heard the bang and the car skidded off the road and onto the grassy verge.

She braked and managed to stop half on, half off the verge but her car had cut out and no matter how much she tried she couldn't get it to restart.

'Perfect!' she said.

She looked in her handbag for her phone but it wasn't there. She had picked it up from the kitchen table and she'd had it when she put on her boots because she'd read a text from a supplier. And then she'd put on her coat, scarf, hat and gloves, and then looked outside.

'Damn it!'

She had left her phone on the hall table. Someone would see it when they went out, but that wouldn't help her now.

She remembered that it was wise to get out of the car but it was freezing outside and this wasn't a motorway, just a B road leading towards one.

She wasn't that far from the village. Maybe a twenty-minute walk. But she'd have to leave her car here and it had just started to rain. No, sleet. No! Snow! Granny had been right.

Now what should she do? Stay here and wait to see if someone drove past and stopped to help? Or start walking back towards the village and get help?

Walking was her only option.

She sighed loudly and was about to get out when a black, Toyota four by four pulled up behind her car.

Rescue had arrived and she thanked her lucky stars until she saw the person who had got out of the other vehicle and was marching towards her front window.

This could not be happening!

What was Griff bloody Betancourt doing

driving up this road?

He tapped on her window and she pressed the button to let it open looking straight ahead as she did so.

'I thought it was your car,' he said. 'What's happened? Have you broken down?'

'No. I thought this was a good spot to stop for a cup of coffee. Of course, I've bloody well broken down.'

He raised his brows. 'Not really the time for attitude, is it, Grace?'

'Oh bugger off. I'd rather take my chances.'

'Why the hostility? I've stopped to help.'

'How utterly gallant of you. What a shame you only choose to play the decent guy when it suits you, and not to actually be one?'

'Erm. I'm not sure what I've said or done to deserve this, Grace. But we can deal with that later. Let's get you home safely first. And in case you haven't noticed, it's snowing out here.'

'I don't want you to get me home safely. I don't want anything from you. I want a car that works. I don't want to see you ever again. Or hear you voice. Or...' She let her voice trail off.

Okay she was taking this a bit too far. Her car had died. She was stuck miles from the village and it was freezing and snowing. Griff had a lovely warm and comfy, four by four that would take her back to her door.

His brows knit together and he looked genuinely hurt by her outburst.

'Then I would suggest you buy a four by four, Grace. Less chance of them coming off the road in bad conditions. And if they do come off the road, they are perfectly happy and will get you back on it.'

'Thanks for that. I will add it to my Christmas list.'

'You should be able to afford one with the money you'll be making from organising the Mistletoe Dance. Although you don't seem to have done much organising after storming off yesterday. Or being stuck out here today. Why is that, Grace?'

'For your information the engine has died.' She didn't mention the fact that she had swerved first and then the engine had cut out once she'd hit the verge. 'And as for the Mistletoe Dance, the rest of the Eversley Events team is at Betancourt as we speak. And if you were there you would know that.'

'Instead, I'm standing here freezing to death in the snow, arguing with you. You're supposed to want to be rescued, Grace. That's the way these things work.'

'I do want to be rescued. Just not by you. If you really want to help. Get back in your car and go and get my dad. He's at your house with the rest of my family. And tell him

I've left my phone at home.'

She faced forward and crossed her arms over her chest.

'This is ridiculous, Grace. Get into my car.'

'No! And don't you dare tell me what to do.'

He glared at her in silence for a moment.

'As tempting as it is right now, I can't leave you out here. If you insist on being this childish, I'll call your dad and wait here with you until he arrives. Don't you have breakdown cover?'

'Yes. But the details are all stored on my phone. And I'm not being childish. This is a matter of principle.'

'Principle? I don't see how. But okay. Although personally, I think calling a tow truck would be a better option than calling your dad. Your choice.'

'Fine. Call a tow truck.'

He took out his phone and stared at the screen.

'Slight problem. I don't seem to have any signal. I can't bear the thought of leaving you out here alone.'

'Don't act like you care. And I'll be fine. I'm a grown woman.'

'Then act like one. Okay. I'll do a deal with you. I'll go and get your dad but you've got to do something for me in return.'

'Like what?'

'Go to Bed and–'

'What!' Her head shot round and her eyes flashed at him. 'Are you insane? Do you really think I'd even consider going to bed with you after … after everything? I'm not going to do that deal and I can't believe you have the nerve to suggest it. But then again, I shouldn't be surprised by anything you do or say, should I?'

His brows shot skywards and he choked for a second or two and the expression on his face was one of shock, followed by disappointment, followed by that sardonic smile of old, and then he took a deep breath and said, 'Well, that was something, wasn't it? I'll try not to take offence at the horror in your voice at the thought of going to bed with me and I won't be upset about your interruption, but I am afraid I must correct you. If you had let me finish, I wasn't suggesting we should sleep together. I was asking if you would go to the shop in Folkestone called Bed and Bath, and help me choose a gift for Davina. She wants some sort of bath bomb set and I have no idea what to look for.'

Grace had never wanted the ground to open up and swallow her more than she did right then. Now what could she say?'

'Fine. I'll go to the shop.'

'That's it? No apology for jumping to the wrong conclusion? Or for casting aspersions on my character? Or for making me stand in the freezing cold and the snow for the last ten minutes?'

'I could ask the same of you. No apology for lying to me and … and leading me on, when all the time you had a girlfriend.'

'What? When did I lie to you? Or lead you on for that matter? You were the one who lied to me. You told me yet again that you love my brother. And I think we both know that's not true. As for my girlfriend. What girlfriend? I don't have one. If you mean Davina, it's not what you think. She's not what you think. Once again you've jumped to the wrong conclusion. She's not my girlfriend. She's a he in fact, and one of my best mates. Davina is her stage name. She's a Drag Queen. But she likes to wind people up. She told Tabby she was my girlfriend as a joke.'

'A he? And …and not your girlfriend?'

'No, Grace? Is that … is that what this has all been about? Is that why you stormed off yesterday? I was furious with you for that. And for throwing that line at me about loving Russell.' He smiled suddenly. 'Were you jealous, Grace?'

'No! Absolutely not.'

'I think you were.'

143

'I don't care what you think. Are you going to take me home? I mean to my home. Not yours. Just in case there's still any lingering doubt.'

Again he raised his brows. 'Erm. I hate to point this out, but a few minutes ago you were never going to see me again or get in my car. Are you saying you've decided you will now?'

'I'm freezing. You're freezing. As you keep saying it's snowing. And getting heavier in case you haven't noticed. We've already wasted a lot of time. I'd still rather not, but it makes sense. I'll come with you and if you'll drop me at home, I can get a tow truck out here.'

'And then you'll come to Bed and Bath with me and help me with that gift?'

'Yes.'

'You're too kind, Grace.'

He shook his head and laughed and then he opened the door of her car and held it while she clambered out. She locked her car with the remote and then they walked in silence to his car, and he opened the passenger door to let her in and then closed it behind her.

He turned in his seat and looked at her. 'I'm still slightly offended that the thought of going to bed with me seems so repulsive to you, Grace. Not today, but one day soon.

Very soon. You and I need to have a serious conversation.'

'Oh? About what?'

She struggled with the seat belt and he reached across and clicked it into place, his arm brushing against her body for a moment and sending a whole new burst of sensations racing through her.

'Do you really need to ask, Grace?'

He started the car and sped off along the road.

Thirteen

'We shouldn't have wasted so much time,' Grace said, a few minutes later as she and Griff peered through his snow-covered windscreen and the wipers groaned under the sheer weight of the sudden heavy snowfall and blizzard conditions.

'And whose fault was that?'

'Granny Joy said this would happen. She said there'd be a blizzard.'

'It might've been helpful if you shared that snippet of information earlier.'

'Watch out for black ice. You can't see it under the snow. There's a lot of it about.'

'Thanks,' he said.

Grace only just spotted the warning road sign.

'There's a bend up ahead. You might want to slow down.'

'I can read road signs too, thanks.'

'Yet you're not slowing down.'

'I'm driving at a sensible speed.'

'Really? It seems a bit fast to me in this weather.'

He stopped the car, swivelled slightly in his seat and slung his left arm onto the back of the passenger seat and looked Grace in the eye. 'Would you like to drive, Grace?'

'Erm. No thanks.'

'Are you sure?'

She nodded. 'Yes.'

'Then is it okay if I continue?'

She nodded again. 'But ... maybe ... just a little slower? I would like to get home in one piece.'

He sucked in a breath and moved the car forward at a slower speed.

At the next bend, she opened her mouth to speak and a little sort of grunt came out. Griff turned his head slightly to look at her, and Grace saw something dart across the road in front of them.

'Look out,' she shouted, and instinctively grabbed for the wheel.

Griff swerved to avoid what appeared to be a fox but in the confusion, the vehicle plunged into a ditch at the edge of the narrow section of road. It was about a foot deep.

'Are we stuck?' Grace asked, as Griff tried to get the vehicle to shift.

'We might be.'

'I told you, you were going too fast. So much for all terrain vehicles being better than my car.'

'This'll cope with almost anything, including driving into a ditch, but driving headfirst into a narrow ditch like this, isn't one of them.'

Nevertheless, he tried. He gunned the engine and the vehicle moved a fraction but not enough to make a difference.

'I can't get enough traction.'

'So we are stuck then?'

'Yes.'

'You could push it out of the ditch, perhaps?' Grace suggested.

He quirked a brow. 'Oh can I? What happened to equality? What would you be doing while I'm using my superhuman strength?'

Grace frowned. 'Steering, of course. Someone needs to make sure it doesn't run away once it's out of the ditch.'

He sniggered at that. 'Sorry. I was just envisioning it growing legs and dashing off.' He coughed and adopted a serious demeanour. 'The ground is flat here, so I don't think it'd go anywhere, but although I'm fairly strong, there's no chance of me budging this an inch on my own.'

'What if I help?'

'Unless you've been hiding some super power all these years, I think that's still a no.'

'Well we've got to do something. We

can't just sit here. We could freeze to death. People do, you know. There's still no signal on your phone, I assume?'

'No. We're not far from home. Probably three or four miles. We could walk.'

'In this weather? Are you mad? We can't see more than six inches in front of us. We could go round in circles. Or ... or walk straight off the cliff!'

'I wasn't suggesting we go now. This blizzard blew in fast. It might blow itself out as quickly.'

'And if it doesn't?'

He looked her in the eye. 'Then I'll go for help. I can use the GPS on my phone.'

'But there's no signal!'

'GPS uses satellites, not mobile phone towers. The blizzard and the surrounding trees shouldn't affect the signal much on my phone, but it's not the same as a map, so it's still not ideal.'

'You can't leave me here alone. What if you get lost? Or worse. What if you fall into another ditch? Or get hurt?'

'I didn't know you cared, Grace.' The triumphant smile on his face was more annoying than his sarcasm.

'I don't. I was thinking about me. If your attempt to get help fails, I could die out here.'

'I see. Fine. Then I think we should wait awhile and see what happens. Another

149

vehicle might come along and spot us.'

'If we're not buried beneath a pile of snow. At least we can use the heater to keep us warm, I suppose.'

'Nope. Unless you like the idea of succumbing to carbon monoxide poisoning. Me? Not so much. We're surrounded by snow, Grace. That means the exhaust is blocked.'

'Then how do we keep warm?'

He turned his head and grinned at her. 'Bodily heat.'

Grace tutted loudly. 'If you think I'm taking my clothes off and pressing my naked body against yours, you're delusional. I've already told you my feelings on that score. I'd rather freeze to death.'

He shifted awkwardly in his seat, glanced at Grace and after a second or two, shook his head and laughed.

'Yet again, you jumped to the wrong conclusion. It's becoming an annoying habit. I wasn't actually suggesting we get naked, but I'm up for it, believe me. I was merely suggesting we huddle together under a blanket. I keep one in the car for emergencies. Don't ask me why. It's just something I do. I like to be prepared.'

He twisted and leant an arm behind him and grabbed the blanket from the back seat. He held it up for Grace to scooch over and looked genuinely hurt when she hesitated.

'Do you think you dislike me so much that you'd rather freeze than cuddle up beside me?'

She met his eyes and held his look for a second. She had already experienced a number of strange sensations by being close to him, and a look or a smile could already turn her insides to jelly. The thought of their bodies pressed against one another was too much to contemplate. But she decided warmth was preferable and that she could control whatever sensations he aroused, so she shuffled across the seat until they were almost touching.

'Keep your hands to yourself, okay? And don't make any sarcastic remarks or clever quips.'

'Okay. But ... I am now wondering if you'd planned this. You know. Make me veer into a ditch just so that you and I could be alone like this.' He grinned as he wrapped an arm around her and pulled her closer.

'I knew it!' She pushed away from him as he laughed.

'Oh come on, Grace. I'm teasing. Surely you can take a joke?'

She glared at him and then to her astonishment he frowned and looked genuinely contrite.

'I'm sorry. That wasn't funny. You're

right. I promise I'll behave. Give me another chance?'

She was wary now. And not just of his teasing. She felt something when his arm wrapped around her and it was stronger than she had expected. For a moment she had felt safe and warm and protected. And also excited.

'You're a jerk. You know that, right?'

He grinned again and nodded. 'Yep. But I really am sorry.'

He held the blanket out enticingly and she gave in and slid back to where she had been. This time he didn't put his arm around her and she was a little disappointed. But she could hear his heartbeat and smell his aftershave and feel the firmness of his body and she closed her eyes and let her mind drift off for a moment.

'Are you comfortable?' His voice was soft and smooth and caring.

'Uh-huh.' She was a lot more than comfortable but she wasn't going to tell him that.

'Grace?'

'Yes.'

He didn't continue so she raised her eyes and met his but she was unprepared for what she saw. His gaze was intense and he looked so serious and yet so unsure of himself.

'I'm sorry,' he eventually said.

'For what?' Grace dare not look up.

'For always being a jerk. For this. For ... everything.'

'This wasn't your fault,' she said, although there seemed to be something stuck in her throat. 'We're in this ditch because of me, so I'm the one who should be sorry. But let's not worry about that. The blizzard will blow itself out, as you said it might and we'll be home and laughing about this before we know it.'

Fourteen

'Why don't you stop bothering me and go and find something more worthwhile to occupy your time?'

As happy as Grace was to be both alive and back on reasonably good terms with Griff, since the morning they had got stuck together in his car in the blizzard, three days ago, something had changed between them.

The snow had melted quickly and the temperature had been far too warm for more snow. The temperature had risen at Betancourt too.

Grace had become more wary of the effect just being close to Griff could have on her. He seemed to have started to tease her again, the way he did when they were young.

The grin on his face curved into a smile and his eyes danced with mischief. 'Am I bothering you, Grace? I do hope so. And frankly, I can't think of anything more worthwhile to occupy my time than ... to *bother* you.'

There was something in the way he said that word, and in the way he was looking at her that sent quivers running all over her body.

She couldn't think of anything to say and if he continued to look at her like that, she wasn't sure what might happen.

Once they had been rescued from Griff's car, by a passing RAC breakdown van and driver, she had dived straight back into work, after explaining to her parents and to Hope about the mistake she had made concerning Davina. Griff was right. Grace did jump to conclusions.

'Next time you think I may be dating someone,' Griff had said, 'or I do or say something that you might've misunderstood, please discuss it with me. Don't dash off and refuse to speak to me. That just makes us both cross.'

He had introduced her to Davina and Grace had seen instantly why Griff and she were best friends. Grace was sure Davina would become someone Grace could be best friends with given the opportunity. Davina had said the same and had winked at Griff.

'Just sayin' honeybun. No pressure or anything.'

Griff had laughed but he had looked at Grace in such a way that made her think she might be seeing more of Davina in the future.

Grace had gone with Griff to Bed and Bath, the shop in Folkestone, as promised, and she had introduced Griff to the joys of bath bombs. He'd bought several sets, not just for Davina but also for Tabby and the staff, and even for Bianca, who was definitely coming home in time for the Mistletoe Dance.

No one was sure what would happen with Archie and Bianca but if Bianca could be in a better head space that might be a start. And maybe take an interest in Archie's new found hobbies. Especially the chickens which the man seemed to adore.

Now as Griff followed Grace from room to room pretending to take notes of things she was saying, of items that needed touching up or finishing or moving or tweaking, she wondered what Griff was waiting for.

Surely if he liked her as more than just a friend, he would tell her? He knew that she had believed herself to be in love with his brother for most of her life, but he had dismissed that as mere fantasy.

Was he concerned about the fact that his dad had loved her mum so desperately? Did he think that might make things difficult? Was he worried about starting a relationship with someone who lived so close? All his previous women had come down with him from London. Did he see Betancourt as a safe haven?

Or was it simply that, although he liked her, he didn't like her enough?

That day of the car breakdown and subsequent accident, he had said that he and she needed to have a serious talk very soon, and yet three days later he had said nothing more about it. He hadn't asked her out. He hadn't told her he liked her more than as just a friend. He hadn't said a word, other than to tease her, just as he was teasing her now.

She turned and swiftly walked away but his footfall was audible behind her and the next second, he grabbed her wrist, slid his hand down to hers and pulled her to him so fast that their bodies thwacked together.

They stared into each other's eyes for a second and then Grace placed her free hand on his chest and tried to push him away.

'Get off me!'

'Don't fight it.'

'What?'

'We have no choice. Look.'

He glanced upwards and Grace's gaze followed his.

Hanging right above their heads was a huge bunch of mistletoe. Grace should've remembered it was there because she was the one who had secured it into position, along with several other bunches of mistletoe dotted around the Great Hall and dining room.

'Don't even think about it,' she warned him.

'I can't seem to think of anything else,' he said, his voice oozing sex appeal.

He bent Grace backwards in an overly dramatic gesture and with a roar of laughter he leant down and kissed her.

It was a playful kiss at first. Just a peck on her lips, but as his soft mouth met hers, something sparked between them and their lips locked into a more intense kiss.

How dare he! How bloody dare he? Grace shrieked silently in her head. How ... Oh God! How delicious!

His arms tightened around her and he eased her upright, pulling her even closer until her breasts were pressed tightly against his hard chest. He deepened the kiss, and moved one hand up her body and into her hair, his fingers caressing and yet possessive.

Grace couldn't stop the moan of desire escaping as his lips teased hers and then the kiss grew deeper still.

'Griff! ... Griff!'

The sound of Russell's voice calling out to his brother, seemed distant at first and then it grew louder and more determined and Grace quickly pushed herself away from

Griff's warm and welcoming body.

Griff stared at her as if he couldn't breathe. As if she had sucked all the oxygen from his lungs and he needed her desperately.

And Grace was also struggling to find her breath. It took all her strength to turn away from him and rush into the hall leading to the kitchen before Russell found Griff and her together. Because it would be obvious to anyone who saw them, what had just happened between them.

She didn't know how she felt about it herself so she didn't want anyone else passing judgement. Not until she knew what might happen from this point forward.

Fifteen

Now that Russell was home there were even more hands-on deck and outstanding items for the Mistletoe Dance were being ticked off the list at lightning speed.

The white poinsettias arrived, along with the pots, and everyone stepped in to tie the pots with ribbons.

The Christmas trees arrived on Saturday, one week before the Mistletoe Dance. Each was manoeuvred into position and dressed as Grace had previously told Griff they would be.

Hanna had finished the trompe l'oeil and the artwork was stunning. Snow covered mountains and forests, frozen lakes and waterfalls, soaring white eagles in the skies and polar bears below on icefields made the trees pop far more than just one big tree.

The wreaths were fixed to the front doors and the silver bells jingled every time the doors were opened.

'Mum would have loved these,' Griff had said when they had arrived, and Russell had agreed, as had Archie.

Grace had taken Griff to the caterers for a tasting and he had been delighted by the food. Most of the food for the Mistletoe Dance was also white, silver, or green, with carved turkey breast being classed as 'white', along with bao buns, and freshly baked bread rolls, but a few exceptions were allowed although they were displayed beneath a camouflage to hide the fact that they didn't comply with the colour scheme. The whole concept was fun and fresh and in line with the winter wonderland theme.

The poles running the length of both sides of the drive had taken time to fix into place, because they had to be secure enough in case of high winds. The lights nets also required securing into place. No one wanted to see a net of lights flying around the village. Some might think it was a spaceship. They ran between the poles like walls of light and across the top, so that they made a tunnel for the guests to walk through, just as Grace had said. The drive itself glistened beneath the glow and seemed to have a sort of ethereal sheen.

Other than the tunnel of lights and the wreaths on the front doors, there were no lights outside at the front of the house, but in the garden at the rear, various lighting techniques had been used to light the lake and fountain, and each of the knot garden, rose garden and other sections.

The copse of trees became a sort of haunted forest and lights outlined the zig-zag path and the raised terrace. Even the ornate gates leading down to the steps which in turn lead to the beach, were lit up.

Back inside the house, each of the rooms had a colour theme to match the colour of the room, so the morning room was lemon and white, the sitting room was red and gold, the drawing room was navy and gold, the kitchen was a rainbow of colours, and so on.

Griff's bedroom, which Grace had arranged with Russell to secretly decorate, was burgundy and cream, and whilst no one was looking, Grace had played at being Goldilocks and had tried out Griff's king size bed. The thought of Griff sleeping beneath those sheets had made Grace think things she knew she shouldn't. she mustn't build up her hopes if Griff wasn't planning to ask her out.

'It's funny isn't it?' said Hope, the day before the Mistletoe Dance, 'Just two weeks and one day ago, Grace was hoping this would be the year her Christmas wish might come true. And now she's hoping it won't.'

'Ah,' said Grace, 'that's not quite true. I

had two Christmas wishes. One was for Russell to ask me to be his date for the Mistletoe Dance, and the other was to wipe that sardonic smile off Griff's face. I'm still hoping at least one of those might come true. And I think you can all guess which one.'

'My Christmas wish might come true,' said Pat smiling at Granny Joy. We got the results of Mum's tests today and it seems she has a tumour on her brain. But no need to panic, the doctor says it's benign and should shrink with treatment and time.'

'We've all got to go sometime,' said Granny Joy. 'I've had a good life and I've been blessed with good friends, and a wonderful family. When my time is up I won't complain. I'll be reunited with my darling husband and all the lovely dogs we've owned over the years. Who could grumble at that? But I'd like to enjoy one more of my darling daughter's Christmas dinners before I go. And a glass or two of Bailey's and maybe some champagne.'

'Cheers to that,' said Hope. 'I don't have any Christmas wishes. What about you, Dad?

'I'm surrounded by mine each and every day. My family are the only thing I've ever wished for.'

'What about you, Lady E?' Grace asked the family dog.

Lady E barked and stuck her nose in the

air.

'I think that means a comfy bed, lots of walks, plenty to eat, and a fresh bowl of water.'

Sixteen

The night of the Mistletoe Dance came all too soon for Grace, and yet not soon enough.

She had found the perfect dress and she couldn't wait to see what, Griff thought of it.

The look in his eyes when she walked in and he took her coat said everything she hoped and needed it to, but his voice said even more.

'You look so beautiful Grace, I don't think I'll be able to take my eyes off you all night. You outshine the stars.'

The dress was fitted to accentuate every line and curve of her body. It was made of the finest silver thread that gave it a gossamer like quality and beneath the see-through silver was the softest white chiffon. She wore her hair in a loose bun and had a single sprig of mistletoe clipped into place.

Griff wore a black tuxedo and a white shirt and cummerbund and his dark ebony hair glistened beneath the lights.

'Dance with me?' he asked as soon as the music started. It was provided by a choir from St Gabriel's Church and a string quartet from Folkestone.

'With pleasure, Grace said, revelling in the feeling of being swept up in his arms and the warmth of his body against hers.

He sighed softly. 'If someone had told me that Bianca's tantrum of just over two weeks ago would have led me to this, I would never have believed them. She looks so well tonight, and that makes this evening even better.'

'She does. And your dad looks happy.'

'Maybe he is. We'll have to wait and see.

He twirled Grace around the floor with dance moves that would have made all four judges of Strictly Come Dancing score them perfect 10s.

'You can dance!' Grace said, surprised at his prowess.

'Why so surprised? It's something I've practiced over the years. If I'm going to do something, I try to do it well.'

She could imagine several things she thought he would do well. He certainly kissed well if that kiss beneath the mistletoe that day was anything to go by.

'I bet you do,' she said.

'Look at me,' he whispered.

Grace almost stumbled when she did.

There was a look in his eyes that made every nerve in her body sing jingle bells at full pelt.

'There's something I want to ask you, but I think Russell has something he needs to say to you first.'

'Russell?' Panic gripped her.

She had been wishing Russell would ask her to be his date for this dance for so long and now, when she didn't want that wish to come true, was this the one night of her life that it would?

'He's going to be waiting for you in the study,' Griff said. 'I'll take you to him after this dance.'

'Griff? Why? What does he want to say to me?'

'I'd better let him say it. It's not my place to do so.'

Was this why Griff hadn't asked her out? Was this why Griff hadn't tried to take things forward? She wanted to run. She flet like Cinderella. Was the magic about to run out?

The music stopped far too soon and Griff held out his arm for her. She reluctantly slipped her hand through it and he led her from the dance floor towards the back of the house to a room overlooking the rear garden.

The moon added an extra sparkle to the water of the lake that was visible through the window. And Russell stood beside the roaring fire of the study, gazing out to the indigo sea beyond, and the black velvet sky dotted with stars.

Seventeen

'You've done a marvellous job here, Grace,' Russell said, looking very handsome but incredibly nervous.

'Thank you. I'm thrilled you are pleased with it.'

'Mum would've loved it too, wouldn't she Griff?'

He glanced over her shoulder to his brother who was leaning nonchalantly against a tall bookcase, his arms crossed loosely in front of his broad chest. He stiffened slightly and his arms dropped to his sides, but he simply nodded and didn't say a word.

Russell let out a long sigh and shook his head. He looked so much like Griff and yet the polar opposite. His blond hair and blue eyes to Griff's ebony hair and dark eyes.

'It's no good,' Russell said, his expression a mixture of determination and fear. 'I can't keep this to myself any longer.'

He was going to say it. Finally, after all these years, Russell Betancourt was going to tell Grace how he felt.

Just when it was the last thing she wanted to hear.

'I love ...' He glanced towards his brother as though seeking Griff's approval.

Please don't give it. Please don't give it. Grace repeated silently in her head and the disappointment when Griff nodded tore through her like a laser guided missile to her heart.

Griff seemed to be avoiding her eyes.

Russell looked back at her and swallowed hard.

'I love Hope!' he blurted out. 'There I've said it.'

Grace stared at him in silence, her mouth open, eyes bulging. She saw Griff push away from the bookcase and move towards them.

'So that happened,' he said, his voice calm as if he wasn't in the least bit surprised by his brother's revelation.

'You ... you love Hope?' Grace queried trying to take this news in. 'Hope? My younger sister? That Hope?'

Russell nodded. 'Have done for years.'

'For years? Wh-why haven't you said anything?' Stupid question. Grace knew that Russell never told anyone what he was feeling. 'Although...?' She shot a look at Griff. 'Did you know?'

He gave a half shrug. 'I'm his brother.'

Grace almost expected him to burst out laughing any second. To make fun of her, or to make some sarcastic remark. Instead a line formed between his brows and there was concern in his eyes, not contempt.

'Are you okay, Grace?'

'I know it's a shock,' Russell said. 'And I know Hope is very different from me. And younger. But not by much. None of that matters when you're in love, does it?' Again he looked at Griff, but Griff was looking at Grace.

'I'm fine,' Grace said. 'Why wouldn't I be? I'm a little ... surprised, but ... I think it's wonderful. I ... I don't know how Hope will feel, of course. And you need to speak to her, Russell, not to me.'

'I shall. I'll do that right now. Only Griff said I should say something to you first. I'm not sure why. But ... you are okay with this, aren't you, Grace? The age-thing, I mean. And the fact we're so different. If Hope says yes, this won't affect our friendship. Yours and mine. We'll still be friends just like we are now.'

He rushed off and Grace watched him go, and then she turned to Griff.

'You knew?'

He met her eyes. 'About my brother being in love with Hope? Or about you not being in love with him despite telling me several times you were, and believing it yourself?' He nodded slowly as he moved closer. 'Yes. I knew how he felt about Hope. Probably before he did, in fact. As for you believing you loved him, as I told you the other day, I've always known.'

Grace sucked in a breath. 'You knew Russell loved my sister but you chose not to tell me? Are you enjoying this? I expect you've laughed your head off over this for the last few weeks.'

He shook his head.

'What did we discuss about you jumping to conclusions, Grace? On the contrary, laughing over this is the last thing I've been doing. As for enjoying it, not one bit. Although I am glad it's finally out in the open. And I didn't say I knew you loved my brother. I said I knew you thought you did. There's a difference, Grace. A big difference.'

'But what if you were wrong? What if I did love Russell? Don't you think that subjecting me to this might have been cruel? It might have broken my heart.'

'I wouldn't have done so if I thought it might. But the thing is, Grace. If I had told you that my brother didn't love you, and that he loved your sister, would you have believed me? You needed to hear it from his own lips. And besides, it wasn't my secret to tell. Do you understand that?'

'Yes. I suppose so.'

'I did convince myself you loved him all those years ago. And I know how it feels to think the person you love, loves someone else. But I knew recently that for some reason, you had still convinced yourself you were in love with one man when in reality, you're in love with another.'

'Wh-what?'

There was a smile on Griff's lips but it wasn't one of his sardonic smiles, it was a caring smile. A happy smile. 'You heard me.'

He reached out and gently touched Grace's ribcage, just below her heart and once again she was astonished by the sensation his touch sent through her.

'Now you're free to be with the man you truly love. The man who loves you back. Who loves you more than he ever thought it was possible to love anyone. The man who has loved you for years.'

'The ... the man who ... loves me?' He nodded slowly. 'From ... from the moment we met?" He nodded again. 'Seriously?' Grace couldn't believe it.

'Yes. Do you really doubt it?'

'Why ... why didn't you say anything?'

'Because you believed you loved my

brother.'

'But why didn't you tell me you had feelings for me? I don't understand.'

'Because I love you, Grace. And love isn't about getting what you want. It's about the one you love getting what they want. You believed you loved Russell, so I kept my feelings to myself. Everything I've done has been to hide my true feelings. I knew how you thought you felt about Russell. If I'd told you I loved you, you'd have pushed me away. And if I'd tried to win you over, you'd have pushed me farther. I know you, Grace. I know what you thought you felt about me. I didn't dare reveal my true feelings. If I had opened the lid on them, everything would have come tumbling out and I'd never have been able to get it all back in.'

'You love me?'

'I love you.'

Grace threw herself into his arms and he kissed her with such passion, and honesty, that she knew he was telling her the truth.

She had convinced herself that she loved Russell, when in reality, it had probably always been Griff. Or maybe she had fallen for Griff over time. Did it really matter?

She loved him now. She loved being in his arms. She loved being kissed by him. She loved the way he looked her. She loved his smile. She loved every inch of the man.

'Well?' he said, when he finally eased away a few inches. 'Are you going to say it? Are you going to tell me I'm right?'

There was laughter in his eyes, but it was the warm and loving kind, and it made her heart soar.

'Don't you have something to ask me first? Like, will you go out with me, Grace?'

He quirked a brow. 'Haven't I just done that? Didn't that kiss tell you how I feel?'

'I want to hear you say it.'

He beamed at her and pulled her closer. 'Then I'll say it. I love you, Grace Eversley. I've loved you from the moment we met and I'll love you till the day we die. Will you please go out with me, Grace?'

'Absolutely, Griff. I thought you'd never ask. What on earth took you so long?'

'Fear of rejection, I think. Or of you jumping to the wrong conclusion. But there is just one thing I'd like to clear up.'

'Oh? What's that?'

'That day you thought I was asking you to go to bed with me, you ... you actually made me think I might've got this all wrong. That the thought of going to bed with me was the last thing on your mind.'

'Don't jump to conclusions. I was cross. To tell you the truth. Going to bed with you has been on my mind a lot. And I can't wait.'

'Seriously? You can't wait?'

'Seriously. I can't wait.'

'You have no idea how long I've wanted to hear you say those words, Grace. But mainly, that you loved me.'

'Then I'll say them again so we're clear. I love you Griff. And I can't wait to go to bed with you. And ... unless you feel we'd be missed. I'd say right now is as good a time as any to start.'

This time, when he kissed her, he swept into his arms and he carried her towards his bedroom. And for the first time in her life, Grace knew for certain that she was exactly where she wanted to be. Not just for Christmas, but for the rest of her life.

Coming soon

Visit www.emilyharvale.com to
see what's coming next.

Plus, sign up for Emily's newsletter, or
join her Facebook group, for all the latest
news about her books.

Stay in touch with
Emily Harvale

If you want to be the first to hear Emily's news, find out about book releases, see covers and maybe chat with other fans, there are a few options for you:

Visit: www.emilyharvale.com

and subscribe to Emily's newsletter via the 'sign me up' box. Or, if you really love Emily's books, apply to join Emily's Open House here:

www.emilyharvale.com/MembersClub

Or ask to join Emily's exclusive Facebook Group here:

www.emilyharvale.com/FacebookGroup

Alternatively, just come and say 'Hello' on social media:

 @EmilyHarvaleWriter

 @EmilyHarvale

 @EmilyHarvale

A Note from Emily

Thank you for reading this book. I really hope it brought a smile to your face. If so, I'd love it if you'd leave a short review on Amazon, or even just a rating.
And, maybe, tell your friends, or mention it on social media.

A little piece of my heart goes into all my books. I can't wait to bring you more stories that I hope will capture your heart, mind and imagination, allowing you to escape into a world of romance in some enticingly beautiful settings.

To see my books, or to sign up for my newsletter, please visit my website. The link is on the previous page.

I love chatting to readers, so pop over to Facebook or Instagram and say, 'Hello'. Or better yet, there's my lovely Facebook group for the latest book news, chats and general book-related fun. Again, you'll find details on the previous page.

Also by Emily Harvale

The Golf Widows' Club
Sailing Solo
Carole Singer's Christmas
Christmas Wishes
A Slippery Slope
The Perfect Christmas Plan
Be Mine
It Takes Two
Bells and Bows on Mistletoe Row

Lizzie Marshall series:
Highland Fling – book 1
Lizzie Marshall's Wedding – book 2

Goldebury Bay series:
Ninety Days of Summer – book 1
Ninety Steps to Summerhill – book 2
Ninety Days to Christmas – book 3

Hideaway Down series:
A Christmas Hideaway – book 1
Catch A Falling Star – book 2
Walking on Sunshine – book 3
Dancing in the Rain – book 4

Hall's Cross series
Deck the Halls – book 1
The Starlight Ball – book 2

Michaelmas Bay series
Christmas Secrets in Snowflake Cove – book 1
Blame it on the Moonlight – book 2

Lily Pond Lane series

The Cottage on Lily Pond Lane – four-part serial
Part One – New beginnings
Part Two – Summer secrets
Part Three – Autumn leaves
Part Four – Trick or treat
Christmas on Lily Pond Lane
Return to Lily Pond Lane
A Wedding on Lily Pond Lane
Secret Wishes and Summer Kisses on Lily Pond Lane

Wyntersleap series

Christmas at Wynter House – Book 1
New Beginnings at Wynter House – Book 2
A Wedding at Wynter House – Book 3
Love is in the Air – spin off

Merriment Bay series

Coming Home to Merriment Bay – Book 1
(four-part serial)
Part One – A Reunion
Part Two – Sparks Fly
Part Three – Christmas
Part Four – Starry Skies
Chasing Moonbeams in Merriment Bay – Book 2
Wedding Bells in Merriment Bay – Book 3

Seahorse Harbour series

Summer at my Sister's – book 1
Christmas at Aunt Elsie's – book 2
Just for Christmas – book 3
Tasty Treats at Seahorse Bites Café – book 4
Dreams and Schemes at The Seahorse Inn – book 5
Weddings and Reunions in Seahorse Harbour – book
6

Clementine Cove series

Christmas at Clementine Cove – book 1
Broken Hearts and Fresh Starts at Cove Café – book
2

Friendships Blossom in Clementine Cove – book 3

Norman Landing series
Saving Christmas – book 1
A not so secret Winter Wedding – book 2
Sunsets and Surprises at Seascape Café – book 3
A Date at the end of The Pier – book 4

Locke Isle series
A Summer Escape – book 1
Christmas on Locke Isle – book 2

Betancourt Bay series
That Mistletoe Moment – book 1
That Winter Night – book 2

To see a complete list of my books, or to sign up for my newsletter, go to www.emilyharvale.com/books

There's also an exclusive Facebook group for fans of my books. www.emilyharvale.com/FacebookGroup

Or scan the QR code below to see all my books on Amazon.

Printed in Great Britain
by Amazon